FAKE IT TRUE

WILD FIRE SERIES

J.H. CROIX

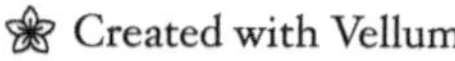 Created with Vellum

Things rarely are as they appear. It's what in your heart that counts.

Chapter One

CASEY HOUSTON

"Couples therapy?" I asked.

"Yes," my mom said. "I just think you need to do that before you completely close this door."

Unfortunately, I wasn't standing beside a wall where I could beat my head against it. I cleared my throat as I bit back the scream bottled inside.

"Okay," I said to my mom. At this moment, I hated loving my family and feeling caught in this god-awful situation where I knew I was letting them down.

"I have the name of a counselor right there in Willow Brook," my mom said. "I understand you've moved to Alaska and this is your life choice. But, please, at least see a counselor a few times so you can make sure you want to leave Nathaniel behind."

"Just text me the information," I told my mom, this time holding back a massive sigh.

Only seconds after I ended the call, my phone vibrated with a text from her with the name of a couples therapist. I could only be so annoyed because I'd completely fabricated a fiancé to keep her off my case. I figured I'd see this therapist to get my mom to shut up about the current bane of my existence.

Nathaniel was the son of my parents' longtime friends. My parents and his were completely oblivious to what an utter asshole he was, not to mention cruel and, in my opinion, responsible for the death of my sister.

As if he knew my mom had just been talking to me about him, a text came through from him. The only reason I hadn't blocked him on all possible channels of communication was I needed to know what he was up to. I collected his texts and never responded.

This one said: *I still don't believe you're engaged. Just remember, we both have a lot to lose.*

———

My eyes dropped down to my bouncing foot as I waited anxiously for the therapist to come out and fetch me for the couples appointment. I was busy formulating some kind of story for why I didn't have my alleged fiancé with me when Leo Massie came out of another office door into the waiting area.

This was one of those shared office buildings with a doctor's office and an accountant here as well. As soon as my eyes clapped on Leo, I knew what to do. "Leo!" I shout-whispered.

His gaze swung toward me, his blue eyes widening. "Hey, Casey, what's up?"

"Remember how you said you owed me something for dumping coffee all over me?" I asked.

His lips quirked at the corners. I ignored the heat that started to roll through me and the way my belly did a little flip, sending sparks scattering through me.

"I do," he said.

"I need you to attend this appointment with me," I was saying as the therapist's office door opened.

"What appointment —" he began.

I leapt up from my chair and grabbed his hand.

"Casey?" the therapist, Delaney, prompted as her eyes arced about the room.

"Right here!" I called.

If Leo had somewhere else to be, he didn't let on and seemed willing to play along with me. Delaney held the door open as she smiled between us. "Come on in."

Leo's hand was warm as it curled around mine. A few minutes later, we'd gone through introductions and were seated on a small sofa. She handed us two clipboards. "If you could both fill these out, I'm going to step into the restroom. I'll be right back."

Delaney left the office. Leo looked down at the form, his eyes scanning it before he glanced to me. "Is this couples therapy?" His brows hitched high.

My cheeks were burning up. "It is. It's a long story. Can you pretend to be my fiancé?"

A long pause followed as his eyes searched my face. "Um," he began.

"Please," I pressed.

He held my gaze for another few beats before he shrugged. "Sure," he replied, swallowing a chuckle.

He looked down at the form and asked, "So why are we here? When and how did we meet, and what do you most love about me?"

My cheeks were burning up, and I couldn't even look at him. I dropped my eyes to the list of questions, ending with, "What are your expectations of couples therapy?"

Leo cleared his throat. "All joking aside, what is happening here, Casey?"

"Premarital couples therapy," I replied, trying not to sound as nervous as I felt.

"I think you're gonna owe me after this," he said under his breath.

"Maybe so, but I really appreciate it."

Delaney returned to the office and sat down in a chair across from us with a warm smile. She stayed quiet while we finished filling out the forms. "Do you need these back?" I asked.

"How about you swap clipboards and see what you think about each other's answers?"

Of Leo's answers, the one that stood out was about what makes a healthy couple. He'd written: honesty, being there for the small things and the big things, feeling safe.

I swallowed through the tightness building in my throat. That was the problem with what my parents hoped for. I would *never* feel safe with Nathaniel. My thoughts spun to my sister and what he had done. I carried her memory like a ton of bricks on my back.

In a split second, I realized I had no idea how to get through this. I'd thought I'd show up for this all breezy and calm and make up some excuse for my fictional fiancé. Even though my mom had found her, I knew Delaney had to protect my confidentiality. With Leo here, I felt like I'd pinned myself under a microscope.

"Are you okay, Casey?" Delaney asked gently.

When I lifted my eyes to her and saw warmth and no judgment contained in her gaze, it was all I could do not to burst into tears. I could brave my way through this as I'd braved my way through life ever since my sister died. I blinked my tears away and lifted my chin. "I am."

I had no idea what to think when Leo reached over for my hand and laced his fingers with mine to give me a reassuring squeeze. There was *no* way he could know the emotional turmoil I was experiencing, but he seemed to sense something.

"So, what brings you two here?"

Chapter Two

LEO

Casey's hand was cold and tightened in mine. It felt as if she was holding onto me as a lifeline at this moment. What started out as pure confusion and amusement when she dragged me into this therapy appointment with her was now followed by a powerful sense of protectiveness. I didn't know the details, but whatever brought Casey into this appointment felt heavy.

I didn't know why she needed someone to pretend to be her fiancé, but I sensed there was a whole bundle of other things going on. I was concerned and wanted to protect her. Now that we were here, I was rolling with it.

I waited for Casey to answer Delaney's question about why *we* were here. Casey squeezed my hand a little tighter and cleared her throat. "Well, um, we're engaged—" Her eyes darted briefly to mine, and I gave her an encouraging squeeze. "To be married," she added. "And, um, everything feels pretty good, but we thought we should come here before, uh, you know..." She circled her hand in the air.

Delaney nodded along, smiling between us. "I can sense that there's a strong connection between you two. Leo, I love that you reached for her hand. Coming to therapy can create a lot of uncertainty, especially in couples therapy. It's a vulnerable space."

"Uh-huh," Casey replied while I nodded.

"Do you mind if I look at your forms?" Delaney asked next.

For the moment, I was engaged and I didn't even know it. My life was normally on the edge of spiraling out of control as a single father, but this might beat that. I felt like I was truly flying blind.

We handed over our clipboards, and Casey didn't let go of my hand. I decided that was just fine. I thought Casey was cute, and we were engaged. I guess. I snorted to myself. For the last year of my life and the insanity that had ensued, a part of me had been thinking I needed to find a good relationship. I didn't know how to be a dad and felt like I was failing at it almost every day, but I didn't want to be *that* guy. The guy who tried to find a woman just so she could take care of my kid. I wanted to feel like I had someone doing this messy life *with* me, but hell if I knew how to find the time for building that with someone.

Delaney quietly reviewed our intake forms. She tapped her finger from one clipboard to the other. "I love that you have a similar answer to what a healthy relationship is."

Since I'd read Casey's responses, I knew we'd both included feeling safe in that answer.

"These are mostly for reference and a way to open a door to thinking about your relationship," Delaney continued. "This answer is important because you're on the same page here. The fact that you're here together, I hope, tells me that you feel safe with each other and safe enough to talk with a therapist."

Casey's hand was shaking a little, and I gave her another reassuring squeeze. My heart smiled a little when she squeezed back.

Delaney launched into a whole thing about confidentiality and how she was treating us as a couple so that would be her focus. "Can you tell me how you got my information?" Delaney asked after all that.

"My mom gave me your name," Casey piped up.

Another detail new to me, although this entire appointment was a bunch of news to me.

I kept on smiling politely.

"Oh, okay, good to know. So, your mom supports you seeing a therapist before you get married," Delaney said.

Casey's auburn ponytail bounced up and down with her nod. "Yep!"

A little while later, we walked out of Delaney's office after we scheduled another appointment next week. I kept waiting for Casey to let go of my hand, but she didn't. We walked all the way out to the parking area. When we got outside, she glanced up, asking, "Which truck is yours?"

"Straight ahead." I stopped behind my truck, glancing down at Casey. "So, uh, that was something," I said.

Her teeth snagged on her bottom lip and awareness sizzled through me. She took a quick breath, letting it out in a rush. "Thank you. I know that was probably strange."

A laugh rustled in my throat. "Something like that. Am I really going to another appointment with you and pretending like we're engaged?"

"You don't have to. I can go by myself. I'll just tell her that the first session was great and thank her for her time."

This was definitely crazy, but my curiosity got the best of me. "I don't mind going to another appointment. How long do you think we can get away with faking it?"

Casey giggled, her cheeks flushing a delectable shade of pink. "I don't know. If you want to go, let's see how long it lasts." She paused before tipping her head to the side. "You don't owe me anything. I spill coffee on myself on the daily."

I held her pretty green gaze for a moment. "It was a lot of coffee..." I shrugged, my words trailing off. "How about this? We do three appointments together. If she still hasn't figured it out, you explain to me why the hell you need a fake fiancé going to counseling with you?"

I could've sworn sadness passed through her gaze, and my heart twisted a little.

She blinked and nodded. "Deal."

Chapter Three

CASEY

When I walked out of my small apartment building, the icy winter air struck my cheeks, instantly invigorating me. I glanced around. Main Street in downtown Willow Brook, Alaska was quiet at 5 a.m. I looked up at the sky as I began walking the short distance. The stars were still bright with just the barest hint of the sun glimmering over the mountains in the distance. The crescent-shaped moon sat low in the sky.

I slipped into the back of the café, locking the door behind me and flicking on the lights in the quiet kitchen. It smelled good, which meant Luna had already been here. Several days a week, she used the kitchen to make batches of donuts. If I could've bottled that smell and sold it, it would be worth millions. It smelled *so* good, lightly sweet and fresh.

I began my morning routine, going out front to fill the display cases, taking the chairs off the tables, and starting a batch of the house coffee for the early-bird customers. After I had everything ready, I made a cup of coffee and sipped on it for a few minutes.

I heard the door in the back open and knew that Luna had arrived to check on her donuts. "Hey, Luna!" I called out over the half-door that led into the kitchen.

She peered over the door, her curly dark hair twisted into a bun high on her head. Her bright blue eyes twinkled with her smile. "Hey! I'm just taking this batch out. Would you like one?" She waggled her brows.

"You know I do."

She grinned and waved me into the back. I followed her with coffee in hand. She knew my favorite, a plain donut with a sprinkling of sugar on it. I slipped my hips onto a stool beside the stainless-steel table in the center of the kitchen.

A moment later, I bit into the warm donut and moaned as the sweet, subtle flavor broke across my tongue. After I finished chewing, I looked over at her. "These are a religious experience."

"I do my best," she teased.

My cell phone vibrated where it sat on the counter nearby. Out of habit, I glanced down. As soon as I saw the text, dread rose inside, tightening my chest.

"Are you okay?" Luna asked.

I swallowed and met her gaze. I wanted to lie and tell her I was, but whenever I got texts from the man responsible for what happened to my sister, I wasn't okay, not at all. I took a quick breath. "My sister died, and I miss her. Sometimes, things remind me of her." That was a serious understatement when it came to Nathaniel.

"Oh, I'm so sorry." Luna slid the tray of donuts she had just pulled out of the oven onto the table.

She stepped behind me and lightly squeezed my shoulders. Luna was generous with her hugs and had a warm, down-to-earth vibe. The first time we met, aside from giving me one of her amazing donuts, she pulled a tarot card for me and told me I'd found my place. I wasn't sure what that meant and was almost afraid to ask her.

She rounded the table to sit across from me. "I want to say something like she lives on in your heart and all that, but that won't take away the grief. Even if she does live on in your heart, which I truly believe, you still miss her," she said, her eyes soft.

I blinked away my tears and took a swallow of my coffee to wash away the scratchy feeling in my throat. "That's exactly it. I know she's in my heart. When you love someone like that, a piece of them is always there. It's not the same as being able to call her up, to hug her, or text her some silly meme that makes us laugh."

Luna was quiet, her eyes understanding. "If there's anything I can do…"

Her words trailed off when I shrugged. "Thank you for listening. It helps a lot to know that somebody understands. Grief can feel lonely sometimes."

I sensed maybe she thought she needed to wait in case I needed to keep talking. "Thank you for listening. I know you have work to do. We're in the awkward conversation moment," I teased lightly.

She rolled her eyes, and I glanced at the clock. "Oh! I need to open!" I exclaimed.

Galvanized, I raced out to the front, calling over my shoulder, "Thank you for the donut!"

As soon as I turned on the lights in front and tapped the button so the open sign was illuminated, a customer came walking in maybe a minute later. I was relieved to be busy. It wasn't as if I would ever reply to that text, but every time I got one, it brought my sister into sharp focus inside. Someday, maybe, I would find a way to tell my parents the whole truth but right now I was busy being fake-engaged after I had fled my small town in coastal North Carolina to come here.

When people asked me why I moved to Alaska, my answer was honest. Alaska was a bucket list place for me.

"Casey!" Janet came into the front and stopped beside me at the counter, curling her arm around my shoulders and giving me a squeeze.

I absolutely loved all the friends I was making here. I couldn't have known it, but the day I drove into town and happened to stop here for coffee was fortuitous. It had been late enough in the evening that Janet had been about to lock up. When I told her I just got into town, she offered me a job on the spot. When I asked for recommendations for a place to stay, planning to crash at a hotel and bleed through my savings, she set me up in her rental apartment next door to the café. She'd leaned across the counter and whispered to me, "I don't advertise it and you look like you need a place to stay."

Inside of the first hour I'd been in town, I had a good job and a cute apartment that was fully furnished. I loved this little town.

When I glanced toward Janet, emotion crashed through me. Maybe it was the text that set off my memories of my sister, fresher than I wished they were, maybe it was the conversation with Luna, or maybe it was just Janet, who was about the kindest person I'd ever met. Janet's motto was she liked her café to feel like a family, but a healthy family. We even had paid leave and health insurance, which kind of shocked me. Janet had explained that she had organized a cooperative nonprofit for insurance where small businesses like hers could sign up and the collective reduced the rate for everyone. Janet was smart and awesome like that.

"Are you okay?" she asked.

My meandering thoughts snapped back to the moment. Now *that* answer was complicated, but I didn't have time to go into it because a group of firefighters came in, and Leo was with them.

"I was just thinking how lucky I am that I stopped here for coffee the night I drove into town and that you let me in even though you were about to close," I replied.

Janet's eyes twinkled as she flicked her silver and black braid off her shoulder. "Well, I am so glad you walked in that night. It worked out for both of us." She nudged me with her elbow and smiled at the group approaching the counter. "All right guys, let's make it efficient. We have some tourists coming in hot behind you."

"Just give me all the donuts," Hudson teased as he stopped at the counter.

"I can't give you all the donuts," Janet said.

"I have four dozen ready," Luna called, peeking over the door with a mischievous smile.

"Luna says you have four dozen," Hudson teased with a brow waggle.

"I know that, but other people like them too, and I like to keep my customers happy," Janet said firmly.

"We understand," Beck chimed in. "Can I carry the box if I pay?"

Janet rolled her eyes with a good-natured grin, and I began getting various coffees ready. The firefighters were all local and usually came in almost every other day. I knew most everyone's preferences.

Leo caught my eye while I was prepping drinks. Janet was getting them various baked goods and Luna was chatting with Beck, who was trying to persuade her to be a personal baker for him and Maisie.

When I had Leo's coffee ready, I passed it across the counter. His fingertips brushed mine when he took it from me. That subtle touch felt like a flame leaping from him to me, scattering sparks over my skin. His blue eyes held mine long enough that heat blazed through me.

"So, I'll see you next week?" His tone was low, just for me to hear.

"Yep!" I chirped. When his lips kicked up at one corner in a half smile, butterflies massed in my belly, spinning in a swirl while my lungs ceased working altogether.

"Casey?" Janet's voice punctured the haze in my thoughts and I jumped. "Um, yeah?"

"Hand me Griffin's coffee," she said, laughter lacing her tone. It was obvious she was repeating herself.

"Oh, right." I hurried to grab it and almost spilled it.

After that cluster of customers left and we handled another

group of tourists, there was a brief lull. I got busy reorganizing the display case and brought fresh baked goods to the front.

Janet was wiping down the counter. She didn't even look my way when she said, "That Leo Massie is a cute one."

My cheeks burned. Conveniently, my hands were full and I could play it off like I was only half paying attention. Janet knew me well enough by now that, if I looked her way, she would know I was crushing on Leo something fierce.

"I think that's part of the job requirements for a hotshot fire-fighter," I quipped as I finished organizing a row of cranberry orange muffins.

Janet chuckled. "Maybe so, but you only get flustered with Leo."

I glanced over at her, narrowing my eyes as I straightened. "Janet." With an empty baking tray held in one hand, I wagged a finger at her with the other. "Don't you even with me."

Her chuckle was sly. "You can have a crush on Leo," she pointed out.

"Janet, I can't have a crush on anyone."

Just when I thought I had the conversation under my control, I went and did the stupid thing. "What do you know about him?"

She practically cackled. Although it was funny, the simple act of being interested in someone like Leo brought anxiety twisting inside of me. Sometimes you learned from your own mistakes and sometimes you learned from the mistakes others made. What happened to my sister taught me a brutal lesson. You *really* didn't know who you could trust, even when you thought you absolutely did.

Janet sobered and studied me. "Are you okay?"

I cleared my throat, striving for a light, teasing tone. "Yeah. Just feeling a little silly that maybe I admitted I had a crush on Leo to you."

She shrugged. "That makes sense. Although Leo just moved back to town, he grew up here. His parents moved away—I think when he was in middle school." She drummed her fingertips on the counter. "They went to Juneau to help take care of his mom's parents. Since his grandparents both passed away, they've been here a lot more. Leo lives in a smaller house on their property that they used to rent out. There is one thing you should know though—" she began.

Before I could ask what she meant, a wall of customers came in. We didn't have another lull in the pace until closing time. By that point, Janet and Luna had left for the day. I was still wondering what Janet thought I should know about Leo.

I was curious enough that I almost texted her but chickened out. I didn't have the nerve to admit just how much I wanted to know.

Chapter Four

LEO

I opened the front door, automatically tossing my keys on the small table beside it and calling out, "Mom?"

She appeared at the end of the hallway, holding her finger over her lips. "She's asleep," my mom mouthed.

I chuckled, my heart tightening a little in my chest. "You know, Dora sleeps like the dead once she actually falls asleep," I pointed out as my mom walked into the living room area.

My mom pressed her lips together. "I know, but sometimes she has trouble falling asleep."

She stopped in front of me, clasping her hands together as she peered up at me. Her once blond hair was silvery white now. Her eyes were still bright blue.

"I am so proud of you for doing this," she said.

"For being the father I should've been all along?" My tone was dry and laced with more than a little bitterness.

She let out a soft sigh. "You know what I mean. You couldn't be a father to a child you didn't know existed, Leo," she said pointedly.

"I know." I was working on the anger I felt toward my ex who never told me she got pregnant. I didn't find out until I got a call from the state's child welfare agency. My ex had given them my name when she was taken to the hospital after a drug overdose.

In a span of twenty-four hours, I went from having no idea I had a child to having a six-year-old daughter. It was an adjustment. An understatement if there ever was one. "Thanks to you and Dad, I can make this work."

"You would find a way to make it work if it weren't for us, but we're so grateful we can help," she replied.

I'd had to make choices on the fly when I found out about my daughter, Dora. I knew I couldn't be a hotshot firefighter forever, but it was my job. My parents were my daycare and more.

When the job opened up here in Willow Brook, I'd had a heartfelt conversation with them when I became an insta-father to a six-year-old girl who had been through more than I could imagine. I was so unaccustomed to being a father that I didn't talk about it much. It was only this morning that I learned from Graham, one of the superintendents on my hotshot crew, that he'd become a single dad straight out of high school after an unplanned pregnancy and his daughter's mom taking off and leaving him with the baby.

He'd told me if I needed any advice to ask him. He'd also offered to babysit if I ever needed help.

I smiled down at my mom. "No need to worry about that. I'm more than grateful to you and Dad. You can actually go home and get some rest," I prompted gently.

"I made you a casserole and prepped some lunches for Dora," she said.

"Mom! You don't have to do everything."

She shrugged. "Leo, I'm retired. Let me be a doting grandmother."

Something between a sigh and a chuckle slipped out. "Thank you for everything." I gave her a quick hug before she left.

Sometimes, life worked itself out. In this case, I was grateful my parents had moved back to Willow Brook when the job opened up for me here. I was also grateful I could live in the old rental property beside their house. This way, I didn't feel like I was bunking in their house, which wouldn't have been horrible, but I wanted my independence. I'd lived on my own ever since I'd graduated from high school.

The convenience of living a five-minute walk from their house made it easy for them to help with Dora. Even better, it meant I didn't have to change jobs. I knew that was a foregone conclusion at some point, but this way when I was out at fires, my daughter's life wasn't too disrupted. As it was, she had already been through more disruption than I wanted to contemplate. I knew I still didn't have the whole story and likely never would because her mom had died.

I walked on quiet steps down the hallway and peered into Dora's bedroom. She was sound asleep with an arm flung over her head and one of her feet poking out from under the covers with her beloved stuffed elephant hugged against her side. The elephant was the first stuffed animal I'd gotten for her. I picked it out the same night I'd learned she'd be coming to stay with me. I'd been in a panic and gone to the local department store to race through the kids' section.

I crossed over to her bed and leaned down to press a kiss on her forehead before I slipped out of the room and closed the door behind me.

Dora was so attached to the elephant she'd named Ellie that she'd cried one day when my mom washed it. Back in Juneau, the child protective worker had referred me to a therapist who helped with the transition. I hadn't told Casey this, seeing as we'd had only one fake therapy session together, but I'd been thinking of trying to get a therapist here for more feedback on how to handle things with Dora.

Although Casey and I definitely weren't even a real couple, I figured I might as well take advantage of the therapy sessions to talk a little bit about Dora. It would fill the time in the appointments.

I laughed under my breath. Casey would eventually find out that I was a single dad, but maybe that detail would dump some ice-cold water on the simmering chemistry between us. Not that I intended to act on it. I had other priorities. There was also whatever the hell Casey's backstory was and why she needed someone to pose as her fiancé.

Chapter Five

CASEY

Every time I remembered that I wanted to get the whole story about Leo from Janet, she wasn't there, or the café was busy. All the while, I scolded myself for being so curious.

Even more ridiculous was the fake engagement therapy situation I'd created out of stupid panic. Ever since I'd dragged Leo into that, I'd realized how stupid it was. I could've just kept on lying to my mother and pretending I was engaged. No one else needed to know. I also could've told her the truth. Except the truth felt way too complicated.

Before our next appointment approached, I realized I didn't even have Leo's phone number to confirm. He came in for coffee on the regular, but it was always busy and I was embarrassed to ask him about it. I didn't want to seem desperate.

You're worrying a lot about feeling desperate, my critical mind taunted me.

"Shut up," I muttered under my breath.

The night before our appointment, I got a little reminder on my phone. As if on cue, my mother called me. While I didn't have much trouble ignoring texts and calls from Nathaniel, I couldn't ignore my mother. I loved her, even though there was a tangled, messy secret between us.

"Hi, Mom!" I injected as much cheer as I could into my voice.

"Hey, sugar," she said in her light southern drawl. "Are you ready to come home yet?"

I cleared my throat. My heart thumped through several achy beats.

"I don't think so, Mom. You know that I always wanted to come to Alaska. I love it here."

Alaska was the last stop in my journey of flight away from my old life and the pain I left behind. This journey had initially started when I felt buried under grief after my sister died. I needed to be somewhere, anywhere, away from a place that reminded me of her every day.

About a year ago, I learned the whole truth about the path that led to her death. I didn't know why, but after I left, my mom got it in her head that if I fell in love with Nathaniel, the son of their closest friends and neighbors, I'd come home. They missed me and she was casting about for a reason for me to come back. It didn't help at all that Nathaniel went along with this asinine idea.

Whenever she brought him up, I would hedge. I'd *never* been interested in him. It went from not being interested to a burning hatred and fear. I was afraid because I recognized how evil he was. He also knew what I knew now. So, I made up a fiancé and cast my sights on Alaska. It had always been a place I wanted to visit, but it became the place for me to escape, to create enough distance.

I'd stopped in Willow Brook that night because I was tired. I wasn't even sure I was going to stay here. Janet made it all possible.

"Are you sure?" my mom prompted.

"Mom, I love Alaska. Leo and I are really happy here." Okay, that was only half a lie.

"Nathaniel is willing to wait for you. It would make everyone so happy for you to come home," she pressed.

I gritted my teeth. "Mom, that's not going to happen. I'm in love with Leo. I'm humoring you and we're seeing a couples therapist before we plan the wedding."

For fuck's sake. My lies were getting out of control. It was crazy enough I made up a fiancé and dragged him into a therapy session with me, but now I was pretending like we were about to plan a wedding. Oh. My. God. I figured I would humor my mom until I found a way to tell her what really happened.

I knew my parents were hurting. It almost felt as if I were betraying them deeply by not staying there. But I couldn't. It reminded me too much of my sister and it always would.

My mother's sigh was quick and sharp. "We would sure love to hear a little bit more about Leo. I wish I could understand why you were being so secretive about him."

"Maybe because you want me to fall in love with someone else," I said dryly. At least, I could be honest about that.

"Okay, okay." My mother sounded resigned. I knew she wasn't going to give up her hopes. Not until she heard the whole story, but that meant blowing up her life, and I *really* didn't want to hurt her. I wanted to protect her from the painful truth.

"So, tell me how you are. Should be pretty hot there by now," I said.

I managed to steer my mother onto updating me on all the things about her daily life. Although there was a part of my heart that would always hold memories of that small coastal town, I also understood life meant accepting change. I'd grown up in my childhood home with my sister and parents on one of the barrier islands in North Carolina. Storms upon more storms were driving the cost of living there up dramatically. My parents were in the process of preparing to move inland. As it was, their home had been renovated twice after nearly being destroyed in storms. Their pending move helped me feel less guilty about the fact that I never planned to live near there again.

Nathaniel's parents lived next door. I didn't like thinking about what he'd done to my sister. I shied away from it over and over. Lately, the news was filled with stories about accidental overdoses. That was technically how my sister died. It was only after Callie died that I learned Nathaniel had been her dealer. I was in possession of reams of texts and more about how he knew he had gotten her hooked, and he kept increasing the ketamine and fentanyl to keep her addicted because that meant more money for him. Until it killed her. I knew she wasn't the only one.

I had to figure out how to make sure the people who contributed to my sister's death could actually be held accountable. After that, I would tell my parents the whole story.

I tried to ignore how good it felt to have Leo's big strong hand holding mine, but it was impossible. He kept doing this thing with his thumb where it would idly brush once or twice along the side of my hand. Each passing touch felt like flames searing over my skin. The heat sizzled up my arm and spun through the rest of my body. I tried to get my pulse to calm down, but it kept racing along like a wild pony kicking up heels in joy.

"So, how was your week?" Delaney asked, her smile warm as she glanced between us.

"It was great!" I practically yelped.

Leo slid his gaze to me before answering like a normal human being with, "Pretty good week."

Our therapist nodded. "Before I check in further, I want to add that when I talk about the concept of homework in between sessions, I don't intend for it to be a requirement. It's more a suggestion."

"Oh, of course," I said, my voice sounding breathless.

"Did you try to have that conversation?" she asked next.

I scrambled mentally, trying to remember what she had suggested. Leo, apparently a better therapy client than me, chimed in, "Oh, do you mean the part about what it meant to feel safe in a relationship?"

She nodded, staying quiet.

I was hot all over. I wasn't sure if it was because Leo was making me hot, or if I was embarrassed because I was doing fake couples therapy with my fake fiancé.

"We did," Leo said, just rolling with it.

Wow, I was really looking forward to his thoughts on this.

"To me, feeling safe is not so much about the good parts. Because those are easy. It's being able to feel like I didn't have a great day and I don't have to pretend for her. It's knowing that she'll be there for me no matter what and feeling like I can be myself with her," he explained.

My head bobbed along, because, of course, that totally made sense. "Yeah," I said when he gave my hand a subtle squeeze. "All of that, and I guess for me, it's also—" I paused, realizing I wanted to give an honest answer, but it was a complicated answer. "Maybe this part is a little different for me because I'm a woman," I began. "But it's important to know that I'm safe-safe."

"Safe-safe?" Delaney prompted, confused by my vague description.

"Well, the world isn't the nicest place for women. Sometimes it's hard to know who to trust. I do trust Leo, so I feel safe with him." I fumbled that explanation, but it was the best I could do for now.

When I felt Leo's thumb brush along the side of my hand, his touch felt soothing, as if he were trying to comfort me.

Our therapist tilted her head to the side, her gaze contemplative. "I think I understand what you mean. I don't expect you to go into detail now, or ever, but I'm curious if someone you know has maybe been hurt in a relationship in a way that's more than just emotional, like abuse." Her tone was gentle.

"Yeah," I said, startled at the amount of emotion that rushed through me. "Leo feels safe for me, and that's really important, along with all of the other things he mentioned."

When she was quiet for a long moment, I started to get worried that she knew we weren't really a couple. Finally, she broke the silence. "Thank you for that. Was there anything in particular the two of you wanted to talk about today?"

Leo took the lead once again. "Yeah. Well, Casey knows I have a daughter. Obviously. She's six years old now."

Holy hell, I had *no* idea he had a daughter. I wondered if this was what Janet meant to tell me days ago now. This was some news. I'd had plenty of practice keeping my expression neutral and hoped I pulled it off. Fortunately, our therapist was mostly focused on Leo.

"Becoming a blended family can be challenging," she said, nodding along.

Leo cleared his throat. "Right, and I'm all she has. Well, me and my parents who live next door and help out a lot. I'm just wondering how I can make this transition as smooth as possible."

Leo squeezed my hand. If he thought I was blowing it, I didn't know because he kept his attention focused on Delaney.

"Do you mind if I ask your daughter's name?" Delaney prompted.

I let out a huge and silent sigh of relief. Whew! She could ask all the questions.

"Dora." He closed his eyes, his shoulders rising and falling with a deep breath before he looked at Delaney again. "I guess you should know the background. Dora's mom died of a drug overdose. It was an accident. She never told me she was pregnant. I never met my daughter until after she died and they called me from the hospital. They revived her with Narcan, but then she became unconscious again and never woke up. Somewhere in the middle of that mess, she told them I was Dora's father. They did DNA testing and, boom, I was officially a dad. Dora felt like an instant child and I'm her only parent." He gave his head a little shake. "It's been a lot."

"That *is* a lot," our therapist said slowly. She glanced toward me. "How do you feel about this? I'm assuming you're comfort-able becoming a stepmother," she prompted.

I nodded, still trying to wrap my mind around this little bombshell.

"I was hoping you could give us some feedback on how I should introduce Dora to Casey. Dora has only been in my life for a little while," Leo added on the heels of a big sigh. "Of course, I've kept Casey updated every step of the way, but it's been as much of a shock for me as it has for her. I only found out about six months ago. Since I travel a lot for my job, Casey and I have lots of long-distance times as it is."

It was certainly a shock. I could tell our therapist was catching on that we had some serious stuff to deal with.

She studied Leo. "I'm impressed with both of you. This is a huge change. When you're in a serious relationship and someone suddenly has a child in their life—" Her focus shifted to me. "And, for you to be supportive of this change isn't easy. It's important to take time to do things carefully."

I was an expert at nodding, so that's what I did. Again.

Leo jumped in, "I've only been back in Willow Brook full-time for the last two months. I thought about introducing Casey to Dora right away, but she's been through so much. Dora, I mean," he added.

Delaney tipped her head to the side. "There's not an instruc-tion manual for things like this. You and Casey are already in a committed relationship and planning to get married. You're doing some of the hard work before you get married by coming to therapy. Even if you only come for a few sessions, I can't tell you how important that is. I'm not saying that therapists solve everything, or have all the answers, because they don't. But the act of seeking feedback is one of the most important skills to have in a long-term relationship. Coming to therapy means you're open to some feedback. As to how to introduce Dora to Casey, my primary suggestion for you would be to do it gradually."

While I sat there, trying to absorb the implications of just how deep this fake relationship was getting in therapy, it struck me that I had no idea how to get out of this now. Unless we just quit coming to therapy, which was maybe the best option.

The session carried along, and we basically managed to bullshit our way through it before we scheduled another appointment. My plan was to tell Leo that I understood this was insane and we could cancel our next appointment. I knew that was maybe a cowardly choice, but he had a lot of priorities and they didn't need to include therapy appointments with me.

After we walked out, we stopped beside my car and I looked up into Leo's eyes. My pulse started to race because that's what it did around Leo. I was formulating what to say when a motion caught the corner of my eye. I glanced over to see our therapist coming out.

"Delaney's coming!" I shout-whispered.

Leo's brows started to hitch up just as I curled my hand into his shirt, tugged him down, and plastered my mouth to his. He made a startled sound against my lips before he got with the program.

Leo's reaction to my unexpected kiss was too much for my system to handle. He slid one arm around my waist and cupped my nape with the other, angled his head to the side, and claimed my mouth.

Sweet hell. He simply took control of the kiss. His tongue swept into my mouth in a slow, sensual tease. I whimpered— what the hell?!—and tightened my fingers in his shirt. I slid my arm around his waist and felt the muscles of his back when they flexed under my touch.

I forgot everything. Who I was, where I was, why I was there. All of it. The only thing flickering in my thoughts was Leo and... *more*.

He gentled our kiss, slowly sliding his hand out of my hair. "Was that good enough?" he whispered against my lips just before he lifted his head.

Shell-shocked, all I could manage in response was a choked gurgle.

Chapter Seven

LEO

My heart was pounding so hard I could feel the echoing reverberation of it in my bones. I could barely breathe, and I was *so* fucking hard for Casey. I knew I had to get a hold of my wits and take a step back.

Her hazel eyes were wide and dark, her lips slightly parted, and her cheeks flushed a delectable shade of pink. As I stared down at her, I noticed the tiny spray of freckles across her nose. Being this close to her only made the lust that had been simmering along flash into fire.

She cleared her throat. "Yes," she whispered.

Her breathy voice kindled the heat burning inside even hotter. It took *all* the discipline I had and the tiniest thread of rational thought to remind myself I needed to create some physical space. I didn't even remember why I started to kiss her.

"Wow," she breathed.

———

Wow.

That single word played on repeat in my thoughts. Casey's kiss nearly slayed me.

I didn't know what the hell to think. It had easily been a year since I'd kissed anyone.

My break up with Dora's mom was old news. Hell, that had been over six years ago. After I found out about Dora, I learned that her mom had also been involved with someone else when we dated. I only found out because her friend had told me the truth. According to the friend, Dora's mom dumped me because she was embarrassed.

I had actually loved Diane. Or, I thought I did. In hindsight, it was hard to know. Being ghosted by her had burned. She'd left town and I'd been stuck wondering what the hell happened.

Now, I knew she'd been pregnant. I let out a quick sigh. According to her friend, Diane panicked. She'd already been seeing someone else. Her friend swore up and down she didn't use anything when she was pregnant. According to Dora's doctor, her development was on track and there were no signs she'd been exposed to opiates when she was in utero.

I knew I would wonder for years about everything. After that break up, which was disorienting because Diane just disappeared, I hadn't been serious with anyone. I'd only casually dated on occasion.

While that kiss with Casey looped through my thoughts, I tried to remember if I'd ever experienced a kiss like that. In plumbing my recollections, nothing shined that sharp and bright. That kiss had felt like a cosmic explosion in my body— two stars colliding and creating a fiery burst.

I also kept wondering why I'd talked about Dora in that therapy appointment. Casey and I weren't real, although that kiss sure felt real.

My curiosity about her kept growing. I wanted to know why she needed to fake a relationship for therapy. Even more than that, I wanted to understand the pain that occasionally flickered in her eyes.

It was late evening when I stopped by Firehouse Café around closing. I was hoping to catch her for a few minutes and talk privately. My timing turned out to be lucky. Just as I reached the door, the open sign turned off. When she saw me through the glass door, she let me in.

"Hey, Casey," I said, as I closed the door behind me.

Her cheeks were pink. "Hey, Leo. Let me lock that." She glanced up with a teasing smile as she added, "I'll make you coffee if you promise not to spill it on me."

I chuckled and followed her over to the counter. "I'll take a coffee, but only if it's no trouble."

"I'll either pour out the rest of the house coffee, or you can have some of it."

"I'll take it."

She started getting it ready for me, glancing over and adding, "I have a leftover ham twist. I know you love those."

"I don't want to make more work for you."

She rolled her pretty eyes. "Leo, all I have to do is toss it in the small toaster to heat it up for you. That's as much work, if not less, than carrying it to the back and wrapping it for the night."

When I nodded, she busied herself with my coffee and getting the ham twist heated up. Quiet fell between us. When she looked up a few moments later and handed me my coffee, the air around us felt weighted with electricity, snapping and crackling. Her fingertips brushed mine as I took the cup from her.

I hadn't thought through what I wanted to say and startled myself. "Look, I don't know why you needed a fake fiancé to go to counseling with you, but it doesn't have to be completely fake."

Casey's eyes widened and a flush rose on her cheeks. Fuck me, Casey blushing was beyond delectable. It was a spur in the flanks of the lust galloping through my body.

She cleared her throat. "What do you mean?"

Well, I was already in this, so I barreled ahead. "I thought you were cute before, and I'm pretty sure I'm not the only one who might want more than a kiss."

She blinked, her blush deepening. "You're not but – " Her words cut off abruptly as she closed her eyes. Opening them again, she stared at me. "I have a lot going on. I don't know what to think."

"It seems like you needed someone for a relationship, fake or not. Everything I said about my daughter is true. Before you go thinking I'm about to ask you to be a mom, I'm not. But we could see how it goes."

She was so quiet for long enough that I was pretty sure I screwed everything up. She lifted her chin. "Okay, let's. As you can tell, I kind of needed somebody to be in a relationship with me."

"Well, I'm already your guy to our therapist," I teased lightly.

Casey sputtered a laugh. "You are. So, um, what now?"

My hand was still curled around the coffee cup on the counter. I lifted it as I leaned over. "We see what happens," I murmured as I brushed my lips over hers.

It literally felt as if a flame flickered between us. My lips felt electrified when I lifted my head. Just as Janet came out from the back.

"Oh!" Janet pressed her hand to her chest, a smile stretching across her face as she looked between us. "Well, I am *very* sorry to interrupt."

Casey's face was fire engine red. She looked from me to Janet. "You are *not* sorry to interrupt."

Janet chuckled. "Not really. I thought you were closed, or I wouldn't have walked out here," she explained. "I'll go in the back now."

She disappeared with a little wave. Casey met my gaze, pressing her lips together and rolling her eyes. "Janet thinks I have a crush on you."

Hearing that was more gratifying than it should've been. My

lips curled into a smile. "I *definitely* have a crush on you. How about I take you to dinner?"

Chapter Eight

CASEY

When Leo asked me out to dinner, all I did was stare at him until he prompted, "Casey?"

I kicked at my brain, ordering it to function.

"Of course! When?"

"Tomorrow."

———

"So you're going to dinner with Leo?" Janet asked the next morning.

Bless her heart, she *had* actually vacated the premises the night before. Which kind of shocked me, but then maybe she hoped Leo and I would get it on in the café. I definitely wouldn't put that past her.

"Yeah," I said, feeling breathless just thinking about it. "I've been meaning to ask you what you wanted to tell me about him."

"In case you didn't know, he has a daughter named Dora. She's six, and he never knew about her until Dora's mother died because she never told him about her."

Seeing as I wasn't ready to tell Janet that I'd set up fake therapy with Leo for some crazy reason that made no sense to anyone other than me, I wasn't ready to tell her that I knew all that. I just nodded.

I was relieved when Josie came striding from the back into the front precisely when a group of customers entered. I could get away with vague responses if Janet wasn't paying too much attention. While I knew the whole story about Leo's situation with his daughter, part of me was a little puzzled that it didn't give me pause. What the hell was I doing going on a date with a single dad? I didn't need extra complications in my messy life.

"Hey!" Josie stopped beside me at the counter, bouncing lightly on her toes. She finished tying her apron around her waist and got to work beside me.

"So, who are you having dinner with?" she asked a few minutes later while we were in the thick of prepping coffees and serving customers.

I slid my gaze to hers, feeling the heat flash into my cheeks. "Oh, so you heard that?" I hedged.

"I sure did." Her eyes were twinkling.

Josie was newly in love with a childhood friend. There was a little drama around it because they'd been cheated on by their respective partners in high school. I personally thought it was perfect karma that they ended up falling in love.

"Leo," I said under my breath.

"Oooooh!" she exclaimed. "Leo is a good guy. I told you a month ago he thought you were cute."

She looked so satisfied with herself I couldn't help but roll my eyes.

She shrugged. "I love being right about love."

"We're having dinner," I protested. "I think talking about love is getting a little ahead of things."

"I like Leo. And he's a single dad. Points for him."

"How do you know that?" I couldn't even restrain my curiosity.

"Uh, Tate. They're firefighters together," she pointed out. "Tate says Leo's great, so he gets my vote."

I snorted. "Well, good. So, if I have more questions about Leo, are you the one I should ask?" I teased.

Josie lifted one shoulder in a light shrug. "I may not be as shameless as Janet, but I'll find out anything I can. My mom usually has the down-low on all the gossip."

Our conversation was interrupted by a large group of customers. I proceeded to obsess about Leo during any spare moment. When I went home that night, I was restless. I tried to watch some distracting TV shows, but nothing sucked me in enough to stop thinking about Leo.

My body kept remembering his kiss while I wondered just what kind of mess I had potentially made for myself. Whenever I started to worry too much about anything, not just Leo, I reminded myself I'd already been through something rough. Surely, in the wheel of random events, I'd get a pass for a little while. My sister had died, and I would miss her for the rest of my life. Worrying about a dinner date didn't rank too high on the list of things to be particularly concerned about. With the tangle of complications I was facing with my sister's death, I knew that I couldn't run away from my problems. They followed me no matter where I went.

Chapter Nine

LEO

"I want to go!" Dora announced, resting her hands on her hips and lifting her chin.

She held my gaze as I looked at her from where I stood beside the couch. She was maybe two feet away, ready to fight this one out.

If you had told me that having a daughter would change my life and that I would love her more than I could imagine loving anyone, ever, in the universe, I would've laughed. And yet, in the short time Dora had been with me, I couldn't imagine life without her now, and I loved her so much it literally hurt sometimes.

"Do you now?" I asked lightly.

She pressed her lips together, a little furrow forming between her brows. Maybe her eyes were the color of mine, but she carried a lot of her mom in her. When she narrowed her eyes, she looked a lot like her mom. She also shared the same glossy dark hair.

I wasn't sure where her feisty attitude came from, although my mom claimed I'd been a pretty opinionated kid. When I saw the glimmer of worry in Dora's gaze, I instantly realized I couldn't tease. Maybe I would never know everything my daughter had been through, but if she wanted to go spend the weekend with my mom and dad on a trip to Juneau, of course I was going to let her go. They were going to a local arts and crafts fair. There wasn't even an iota of doubt I'd support her going.

"You're going," I said quickly. "You definitely don't need to worry about that."

Dora's shoulders dropped when she let her breath out dramatically. "Oh, goody! Grammy said I had to ask you."

The tension around my heart eased a little when Dora beamed and that glimmer of worry disappeared from her eyes. She squealed, "Yay!" before flinging herself toward me and wrapping her arms around my waist.

I squeezed her tight and let her go. It was hard to describe the emotional joy I felt whenever she hugged me. It was also fascinating to observe just how much a child lived in the moment. Seconds after that, all worry dissipated, she announced, "And, tonight I have a dinner party with Grammy."

I bit back a chuckle. I'd told my mom I was meeting friends for dinner. I think she assumed I was having dinner with the guys on my crew because I did that once a week or so. If my mom knew I was having dinner with a woman and the whole story behind it, she would be freaking right the hell out and asking five million questions.

"Are you planning to help with dinner?" I asked.

My daughter was all business now and nodded. "I'm gonna make a sugar cake. Grammy is gonna let me do stuff in the kitchen."

I tweaked her ponytail as I walked by. "Sounds like fun."

Dora paused as she reached for her jacket hanging on the small row of hooks I'd put there just for her. Below the hooks were some cubbies where she kept her boots, mittens, and other winter gear. Her gaze sobered as she looked up at me. "Are you gonna be lonely tonight?"

I smiled down at her with my heart twisting sharply in my

chest. "I'll be okay, I promise. Since you have plans, I'll call my friends and we'll do something for dinner."

"Okay," she said solemnly, just as there was a light knock on the door.

My mom knew Dora loved answering the door, so she humored her by making a show of it. Dora put her hand on the doorknob, calling through, "Who is it?" in a singsong voice.

"It's Grammy!"

Dora flung the door open, giggling. My mom lifted her, spinning her in a circle before giving her a hug and setting her back on the floor. "Are we ready to go?"

"Yes!" Dora exclaimed even though she didn't have any shoes on yet.

My mom looked around and then out on the porch, asking, "Do you need shoes for your walk?"

Dora giggled again and hurried to put them on. Moments later, they were walking down the stairs hand in hand.

———

"Have you been here before?" Casey asked as she leaned back in her chair before looking around the small café in the local art gallery.

"I've gotten takeout from here, but I haven't actually sat down here."

"Same. I think it's so cool that they rotate their menu. This month is an Indian cuisine theme, and I'm so excited! They have a buffet and everything." She paused, her eyes twinkling. "Can we just get the buffet? I love a buffet."

I chuckled. "Sounds good to me. Were you worried I wouldn't want that?"

Her cheeks turned a little pink. "I didn't know. And, I should ask now, are we splitting the check? I don't want that to be awkward."

"Since I asked you out to dinner, I presumed I would be

paying. But I don't really know the rules for dating these days. I haven't gone on a dinner date in... Well, a while."

Casey was quiet as she held my gaze. She began nibbling her bottom lip with her teeth. I didn't think she was intending to be sexy and cute, but pretty much everything Casey did was sexy and cute, so I had to try to stay focused while lust revved its engine.

"I don't know what the rules are either. You're welcome to cover dinner. I guess if we go on another dinner date, I'll get it," she finally said.

"It doesn't have to be even. Life isn't really like that."

"I know." She lifted one shoulder in a shrug. "I was just offering."

A sense of nervousness slid through me, and I rested my elbows on the table.

"Neither one of us has dated in a little while," she pointed out.

"Seems to be the case," I replied. "What's your reason?"

Casey blinked, an intense pain flashing through her eyes that sent a jolt of protectiveness through me. She glanced away quickly to unroll the silverware from its napkin.

A moment later, a waiter arrived. Beyond each of us choosing water to drink, he delivered plates for the buffet. We loaded up before returning to our table to sit down. I was wondering if Casey was going to let the topic of dating drop, and I didn't want to pressure her. I knew there was a story, if only because she needed someone to pretend to be engaged to her.

After a few bites, she glanced over. "I guess maybe you might want an explanation for why I dragged you into a therapy session as my fake fiancé."

I cocked my head to the side. "You don't owe me an explanation, but I'm definitely curious."

Her lips quirked in a sad smile. "To make a complicated story simple, my parents would like me to fall in love with the son of their best friends. I was trying to be vague, but I ended up telling my mom I was engaged because the guy in question is a total asshole. I want nothing to do with him. Ever. But it's awkward because..." She circled her hand in the air.

"Close family friend, and all that," I offered.

She looked sheepish when she shrugged. "Pretty much. My mom somehow got this therapist's name and wanted me to go to therapy with, well, my fiancé, just to make sure we knew it was the right thing. I saw you in the waiting room, one thing led to the next and now we're having dinner."

I nodded slowly as we stared at each other. It felt like the air before a storm, weighted with electricity humming.

I wanted to ask who hurt her, what lay behind the pain I saw in her eyes. My gut told me that maybe pushing her on that tonight wasn't wise.

"What about you?" she prompted.

"The next logical question," I said dryly. "You heard most of it in our appointment. Dora's mom and I dated. Years ago. She broke up with me by ghosting me. Just completely fell off the radar and moved out of the area. That burned even though it let me know I wouldn't want to stay with her anyway. I didn't hear from her for over six years. And then, I got a call about Dora."

Casey's lips twisted to the side as anger flashed in her gaze. "She didn't even tell you she was pregnant, right?"

"Nope. I've since heard from a mutual friend that we had back when we dated that she'd been seeing someone else behind my back. Her friend claimed she wasn't sure who the father was. I don't know if I ever would've found out about Dora if her mom hadn't died."

My feelings about Diane were complicated. There was the bitterness I felt after being ghosted by someone I thought I loved, followed by so much unfinished business. Now, my primary concern was Dora and making sure she was okay. I wanted her to be better than okay, and I didn't know how to make sure that happened.

When I looked into Casey's eyes, the empathy there almost

hurt to see. "That wasn't fair to you, or to Dora. I'm really sorry you went through that."

I took a breath. "Same here. So, after what happened with Diane, I haven't really dated. I haven't been a monk, but I haven't really trusted anyone, I guess. Being ghosted completely bites. I definitely know what it means not to trust someone."

We ate for another minute or two before Casey asked, "How did you find out what happened?"

"When the social worker from the hospital called me. Hadn't heard a thing until then. From what I understand from her friend, she was pregnant when she broke it off with me and I guess she thought the other guy might be the father."

Casey pressed a palm to her chest, her eyes glistening with tears. "I am so sorry. Do you know what happened to the guy she thought was Dora's dad?"

"According to Diane's friend, they broke it off not long after she had Dora. He didn't want anything to do with raising a kid." I took a quick breath, letting it out. "I'm obviously sorry for everything Diane went through. I am really fucking glad I'm not trying to deal with Dora being attached to some other man who was a father figure to her. I wouldn't want the emotional mess that comes with that."

"I totally understand." Casey nodded vigorously. "That would be tricky."

A bitter laugh rustled in my throat. "That it would."

The waiter came to check on us and our conversation moved away from the loaded topic of dating, or rather, lack of it. The question I couldn't even answer inside my own brain was why I was doing this with Casey. Obviously, there was a spark. Hell, it more like a raging bonfire.

I didn't want to dwell on that. The more I spent time with Casey, the more I liked her. I told myself we could keep it neat and tidy, not complicated.

Chapter Ten

CASEY

Why did you have Leo pick you up? This is a really bad idea.

My hormones were behaving like a rowdy teenager. They ignored all of my caution. My hormones wanted Leo, wanted another kiss, wanted *more* than a kiss.

Somehow, during dinner, I talked myself into this little corner in my mind where it was totally okay for us to casually date even though he had a daughter and my life was a mess. But I trusted Leo, and wasn't *that* something?

In the years since my sister Callie had died, trust had felt nearly impossible to find. I trusted my parents. And yet, I'd broken their trust by keeping a secret that would tear them to pieces if they knew it. I didn't know what to do, or how to sort it out. I didn't know who else knew what had been going on with Nathaniel and Callie.

I'd always wanted to travel. After Callie died, I wanted to run away, so I did. Two birds, one stone. I would scratch my travel itch and escape the mess that I felt powerless to clean up. Now, it felt like one lie was rolling into the next, and here I was on a date with my fake fiancé. The fake fiancé who nobody even knew was my fiancé here. Complications were adding up by the day.

My attention narrowed to a singular focus when Leo walked me into my apartment building. I should've run out of the truck. But when he offered to walk me up, my rowdy hormones were all, "Hell, yeah!"

The downstairs of the building had a larger apartment that Janet rented to tourists. The upstairs had two apartments with mine on one side and an empty one on the other.

Our footsteps sounded loud to my ears as we walked up the stairs and turned down the hallway. I had a doormat with a sunflower on it in front of my door.

Leo glanced down at it, his lips twitching with a smile. "That suits you."

"A sunflower?"

"Yeah. Cheerful and pretty, like you."

The simple compliment startled me, and I smiled before I could get embarrassed. "Oh! Well, that's sweet of you."

His baby blues held mine as his lips kicked up at one corner before his smile stretched to the other. Heat pooled low in my belly, and I suddenly felt breathless as I looked up at him.

He rested a hand on the wall beside my shoulder before he startled me with his blunt words. "I want to kiss you again, Casey." He closed his eyes briefly as he shook his head. When he opened them again, the blue had darkened to almost navy. "I want to do a lot more than kiss you." He released a sharp breath. "But I don't know what you want."

"You already know my life is a little complicated," I said while my hormones did cartwheels inside and I tried to ignore the joy buzzing in my veins.

"I definitely understand complicated. Maybe we just see what happens. We don't have to tell everybody we're engaged," Leo replied.

"And going to fake couples counseling," I offered, my tone dry as burnt toast.

Chapter Eleven

LEO

Casey giggled, and the sound sizzled through me. She was so damn endearing.

"Maybe that's a good idea," I rasped.

"What?"

"We see what happens. Tell me what you want."

"Now?" she whispered.

Holy hell, the sound of her breathy voice was like pouring gas on a raging fire.

"Yes, now."

She placed her palm on my chest as she leaned up, sliding her other hand around the back of my neck and pulling me close. When our lips met, it felt like lightning striking between us, sizzling and burning hot.

In a matter of seconds, our kiss went from a hot shock to wild and messy. I absolutely could *not* get enough of her. The way she tasted a little sweet, the way her scent carried hints of the crisp air outside, and the way she kissed boldly and without reservation. Her tongue glided against mine in a sensual tease. She made this whimpering sound in the back of her throat and flexed into me. I could feel the tight peaks of her nipples through her cotton blouse.

My cock swelled to the point of pain. When she rocked her hips into mine, I couldn't help but rock with her.

Casey let out a gasp and her head fell back against the wall when we broke apart. It felt as if she was imprinted on me, all lush softness and warmth. We stared at each other in the quiet hallway. I could hear the drumming beat of my heart reverberating through my entire body.

"Oh, wow," she said on the heels of a shaky breath.

It was all I could do not to lean close and claim her mouth again. She took in a slow breath, the air gusting against my cheek seconds later. Just when I thought I'd gathered up some semblance of control, she leaned forward and pressed her lips in the divot at the base of my throat. When she drew away, her eyes were like fire.

"Kiss me," she commanded, her voice low and throaty.

Our mouths collided, and once again, we dove into a devouring kiss. I savored the warm sweetness of her mouth and every little whimpering sound she made. My knee slid between her thighs and she rocked her hips over it. Our kisses blurred from one to the next. The next thing I knew, her head thumped against the wall behind her again as she shuddered all over, finding her release right there in the hallway with us both fully clothed.

Her eyes were heavy-lidded as she stared back at me a few seconds later, both of us sucking in deep gulps of air. "I need to taste you," I whispered.

Chapter Twelve

CASEY

I need to taste you.

I blinked in response to Leo's words. All I could manage in reply was a wobbly nod.

I wasn't sure what he meant, but when he unbuttoned my jeans and slid his hand between my thighs to dip his fingers in my slippery wet channel, my pussy clenched around him. I was still reverberating from the echoes of my unexpected climax.

When he withdrew his fingers, with his eyes on me the entire time, he brought them to his mouth. I thought I might melt to the floor right there. I watched on weak knees as he licked my arousal off his fingers. I distantly heard the sound of my choked whimper.

The friction created from his knee had been enough of a shock, but watching this sent another burst of need through me. All I could do was try to breathe.

A moment later, he buttoned my jeans. It slowly dawned on me that we were in the hallway. I knew there was nobody in the apartment across from mine, but still. I had completely lost track of where we were.

Leo gave me a lingering kiss before stepping back. When I

lost the feel of his body against mine, I felt bereft. I wanted to yank him back.

On unsteady knees, I pushed away from the wall and fumbled for my keys. He waited until I opened the door and stepped into my apartment before saying, "Good night."

I clung to a slender thread of reason and managed to tell him good night before closing the door and locking it behind me. I heard his footsteps retreating down the hallway and stairs before I stumbled across the room and collapsed on the couch.

"Oh, my God," I whispered to myself.

———

"Well?" Josie asked the following day. Her unruly brown curls were tamed into a ponytail as she smiled at me.

"Well, what?" I hedged.

Josie's brows hitched up. "Your dinner date, although I know it went well because you blushed as soon as I asked."

My face had to be fire engine red by this point. "You just said "well"," I protested.

She burst out laughing as she turned to begin prepping our coffee. I loved it when Josie and I opened the café together. We always arrived early. She made us coffee and we heated up left-over baked goods from the day before.

"Hello!" Luna's singsong greeting carried from the back. When Luna was here early, we usually got a fresh donut from her.

"Hey!" Josie and I said in unison.

"I'll make enough coffee for you," Josie added when Luna peered over the half door behind the register. "I was just asking Casey how her dinner date with Leo went."

"Josie!" I was pretty sure my face was going to melt off at this point.

Luna caught my eyes and waggled her brows. "Clearly, it went well." She waved us into the back. "Come in the back while I deal with the donuts."

We followed her, and I let out a sigh as I looked between my friends. Luna began sliding trays of already prepped donuts out of the refrigerator, and I walked over to help her. "I'll start the oven?" I prompted.

"Sure thing."

"Set it at four hundred degrees?" I asked.

Luna flashed me a quick smile with her nod. "Pretty soon you're gonna be able to bake these yourself."

I burst out laughing. "I don't think so. Even though I know the temperature, it's your magic recipe. My baking skills are average, not amazing like yours."

A few minutes later, the three of us sat on stools around the stainless-steel table in the kitchen. We were sipping coffee and chatting.

"So, you never did answer me," Josie pointed out as her perceptive gaze held mine.

I felt a little self-conscious and delayed a few seconds by taking a swallow of my coffee. When I set the mug down, I took a deep breath for courage. "It was really nice. I haven't actually had like a date in, well, I don't know, a long time." A rush of sadness rose inside, and I suddenly wanted to cry.

Luna sensed my distress and leaned over from where she sat beside me, curling her arm around my shoulders and giving me a quick squeeze.

"Are you okay?" Josie's eyes were concerned as she studied me from across the table.

"I'm fine. We actually talked about the fact that neither one of us has dated in years. Leo has his own trust issues because of his ex and..." I paused to gather myself. Even though I wasn't planning to, I spilled the whole story about what happened to my sister, finishing with, "And, I hate Nathaniel. So much. There's no way to ever really prove what happened, but I know it did. It blew my world up. It isn't just that my sister died. Because that will hurt for the rest of my life. Even though I didn't really trust him, I guess I never thought Nathaniel could do something like that. My parents don't know. They want me to give him a chance. He's bullshitting them, telling them he always had a thing for me. Since Callie died, they've just been devastated." When I looked between my friends and saw the combination of sadness and horror on their faces, I rushed to apologize. "I didn't mean to ruin the morning. I'm sorry."

Josie leaned forward, setting her coffee down as she held my gaze. "You do *not* need to apologize. You're living with this every day. Part of being friends is telling each other what we're going through. I can't believe that happened to your sister. I knew she passed away, but, oh, my God, no wonder it's hard for you to trust."

Luna looked pained, her eyes glistening with tears. "I am so sorry. I want to light that man's life on fire."

Tears stung my eyes again. This time the sadness was still there, but it helped so much not to be carrying this alone. "Thank you. Sometimes it feels really lonely, and I haven't felt safe telling anyone what happened."

"If there is *anything* we can do, we'll do it," Josie said, her voice fierce.

"I know." When I smiled between them, it was bittersweet. "I don't really think there's anything I can do about what Nathaniel did, and I can't bring my sister back." I paused to take a deep breath. "Having a good dinner date with Leo brought all that up," I offered, trying to lighten the moment.

Josie's smile was warm. "Makes sense. You haven't really trusted anyone."

"Do you trust Leo?" Luna asked.

I pondered for a moment, doing a body check, but I was nodding without really thinking about it. "I do. I really do."

That was kind of a big deal. We didn't get a chance to talk more because opening time rolled up fast.

I thought about Leo that night when I got home. I loved my little apartment and how safe it felt. It was cozy, and it was mine.

I turned on the television and snuggled up in my favorite blanket on the small loveseat. I had a big mug of hot chocolate with marshmallows and a donut from Luna. She'd tied it up with a bow for me.

I was wondering when I might see Leo again when my cell phone vibrated with a text. I reached for it, glancing at the screen to instantly feel nausea rising in my throat.

"Fuck you, Nathaniel," I muttered as I stared at the screen.

Nathaniel: You can't avoid me forever. I don't know what you think happened, but I know it's not what you think.

I left him on unread. That's how I left all of his messages.

I took a swallow of my hot cocoa, trying to will away the anxiety that instantly began whirring like a storm in my chest.

"It didn't matter," I whispered to myself.

Callie was never going to come back. I had nothing to lose other than to destroy their peace of mind by telling my parents what happened.

My mind scurried about, trying to think about anything other than this. I did have one perfect distraction.

Instead of waiting for Leo to text me, I texted him. Which was so wildly out of character for me that I got flustered as soon as I hit send. Glancing down, I reread what I wrote.

Me: Hey, was wondering how you're doing.

"Oh, my God," I muttered to myself. "That's stupid."

I had never been one of those people who was quick and witty when it came to texting. That kind of communication didn't come naturally to me. Before I had a chance to berate myself for too long, my phone vibrated. When I saw Leo's name flash on the screen, my lips curled into a smile. If my belly had been a hula girl, she would've been dancing and twirling her skirt.

Leo: I was wondering the same thing. I want to see you again.

Me: We have our therapy appointment on Tuesday.

As soon as I hit send, I again felt ridiculous. I was pretty sure he wasn't talking about wanting to see me in therapy.

Leo: Of course, I'm looking forward to that, but I meant another kind of seeing you. 🌙 Dora will be out of town next weekend. I'd love to take you out to dinner again.

"Oh, my God, oh, my God, oh, my God."

I had to force myself to breathe. "Calm down," I ordered myself.

Leo elicited a new level of talking to myself.

I took several deep breaths and closed my eyes. After I thought I had it under control and could text like a normal person, I lifted my phone again. I was sitting by myself in my tiny apartment with my pulse rampaging out of control and my belly doing gymnastics while I was texting with a cute guy.

Me: I'd love that!

Before I meant to, I hit send by accident.

"Oh, my God. Fuck my life," I muttered.

"Fuck your life?"

I yelped, looking around wildly and almost tumbling off the sofa out of panic when I heard Leo's voice.

"Leo?" I squeaked.

"Yeah. You called me." I could hear the laughter lacing his voice.

My cheeks were burning up. Well, *all* of me was on fire.

"I think I hit the call button by accident. You know how the text window has the buttons where you can call and—" I started babbling before I snapped my mouth shut. On the heels of a deep breath, I added, "I said "fuck my life" because I was embarrassed that I said I'd love that. If you didn't know, I'm not cool. I'm not cool *at all*. I'm not quick or witty or anything like that, especially not over text."

Leo was silent for a moment before he replied, "Casey, I didn't ask you out to dinner because I thought you were cool. I like you. It's as simple as that."

When he chuckled, the sound spun around my heart, soothing the anxiety rising fast inside. "Well, that's a relief."

"I'm just relieved you weren't saying "fuck my life" because I asked you out to dinner again."

"Definitely not," I said flatly. I sat there, holding the phone to my ear, smiling and feeling silly and safe.

"So, about dinner?" Leo prompted.

"I'd love that. Really."

"And, remind me when our therapy appointment is," he prompted. "I forgot to write it down."

For a second, I wanted to tell him it wasn't necessary for him to go anymore. I knew my parents could never find out whether I had a fiancé and if we were going to therapy. But I actually liked those appointments with him.

For once in my life, I didn't overthink something. "It's Tuesday in the afternoon at two."

"I'll see you there."

I didn't really remember what else we said. It was only later that night when I was falling asleep that I realized I had completely forgotten to dwell on my anxiety around Nathaniel and what happened to my sister.

Chapter Thirteen

CASEY

"Callie was a year older than me. Before she died, I knew something was wrong. She started dating this guy and the next thing I knew she was being really squirrely. She ended up breaking up with that guy. Even though I wasn't hearing from her as often as I usually did, I hoped for the best. I couldn't expect her to report back to me all the time. When I went to visit her one weekend, I found out she was dating Nathaniel. Nathaniel's parents are really close to ours. We grew up together. To be honest, I never trusted him, he always came off as selfish to me. He's been a part of our family life for years. We did holidays together, dinners, and so on." I circled my hand in the air. "I started getting really worried about Callie. She played soccer in college and injured her knee pretty badly. That's when she got hooked on pain meds. When the doctor stopped prescribing them, she found them in other places. The weekend before she died, she told me about that. She was embarrassed and said she wanted to get help, but she made me promise not to tell our parents." My words came out in a flat tone. I kept the pain of my grief locked up so tight, I felt compressed inside whenever I tried to talk about it.

I took a slow breath. "It was too late. I didn't know that

Nathaniel and another guy were her dealers. They were giving her stronger and stronger stuff. The more addicted somebody is, the more money they spend." I hadn't realized tears were rolling down my cheeks until our therapist gently nudged a box of tissues closer to me on the coffee table. Leo was holding my hand, and his thumb brushed in a soothing stroke across the back of it.

"The hospital said it was an accidental overdose. They said Callie could've been saved if she'd had emergency medical treatment sooner, and they asked me if I knew where she got her drugs. I know, and I'm pretty sure if I do anything about it it'll tear my family apart."

I hadn't walked into this office today intending to dump the whole story about my sister, but I felt safe with Leo. When Delaney asked me something, everything started to spill out. This was the first time I'd outlined the whole story to anyone. Up to this point, I'd collected the details and kept them tucked away in my own thoughts. The few times I'd spoken of the events, I'd kept the details vague.

I took another breath, letting it out in a deep sigh that felt like it came from the bottom of my feet. Delaney's gaze was kind. "I'm so sorry," she said softly. "I realize those words often feel inadequate, but sometimes all we can do is bear witness. Your pain and your loss are real."

Leo's voice was gruff when he said, "I'm sorry."

Every so often, I wondered how obvious it was that Leo and I were telling our stories to each other for the first time. And yet, we were being honest. It was a testament to our therapist's skills that she had created this space of safety, even though it had started out not-so-honestly for us. Maybe she sensed that, but I found it didn't really matter to me anymore.

Delaney glanced between Leo and me, adding, "You've both experienced a loss due to accidental overdoses. I'm sure you don't need me to tell you those are shockingly common these days."

"Oh, I've looked up the stats," Leo offered. "It's devastating."

Delaney nodded before bringing her attention back to me. I clung to Leo's hand like a lifeline. You would've had to pry my grip free from his at this point. His strong presence was calming and soothing.

"You're not asking me, but I imagine you're wondering what you should do about what you know," she prompted.

My heart ached with every beat whenever I thought about what happened to Callie. "I don't know how to prove Nathaniel's involvement. I don't even know if it's worth trying."

"I tend to think secrets out themselves. Eventually," Leo offered, his tone low and clear. "I mean, obviously the details are completely different, but it's like my daughter. I wish it had happened differently, but I'm pretty confident I eventually would've found out about Dora one way or another. With the Internet, it's really hard for secrets to stay secret."

I savored the feel of his thumb idly tracing over the back of my hand. Our therapist was quiet for a beat before she offered, "When I do family therapy, I always tell families if they have any secrets, they'd better be prepared to discover that what they think is a secret isn't actually. It's not so much that people know all the details. But when people care about each other, they know when something is being hidden on some level. If that makes any sense. Separate from legal consequences for Nathaniel, you might want to think about how to talk with your parents. If they found out another way, their sense of devastation may run deeper because they will have unintentionally taken part in caring about someone whose actions contributed to Callie's death."

Once again, I didn't realize tears were splashing onto my cheeks until Leo leaned over and fetched the entire box of tissues before handing me a fistful of them.

That was the kicker. My parents were close to someone who made Callie's addiction worse. I knew eventually I would need to tell them the whole story. I just didn't know how to go about doing that.

"My concern for you is this will weigh on you until you let them know everything," Delaney said.

"I know. That's why it's so hard. I need to figure out how to tell them."

Leo squeezed my hand. I looked up into his eyes before turning back to Delaney. "Thank you," I said softly.

Her brows hitched up in question.

"For listening, for making space so that I could talk about all of that," I added.

She looked between us. "Like I told you back when we first met, not every therapist is for everybody, but I'm glad you feel comfortable with me. If that's all I manage to do, I consider that a success."

I took a shaky breath and dabbed at my eyes. I knew our time was almost up. Rather than waiting for her to figure out how to gracefully exit this conversation, I piped up, "Don't worry about putting me back together. This isn't a new story. It's been a relief just to talk about it."

She nodded. "You have each other. It's obvious you're both supportive of each other. I would just remind you, as I do in every session, when something painful comes up, be gentle with yourself."

We scheduled our next appointment. When Delaney was entering it into her calendar, I glanced over at Leo. It was no more than a few seconds, but when my gaze snagged his, the moment felt intensely emotional.

Chapter Fourteen

LEO

That afternoon, I went to the station to work out. My mind was still reeling from our therapy appointment. The pain in Casey's voice had felt like knives dragging across my heart. I'd wanted to do more than hold her hand. I'd wanted to wrap her close and comfort her and protect her from all that pain.

I was wrestling with anger toward the man who had caused her so much pain. While the details were so different, I understood what it was like to lose someone that way and the muddied sadness that came with it.

The news was filled with stories about the scourge of society that opiates had become. Many people understood it on a deeply personal level.

I was leaving the workout room and encountered Graham walking down the hall just as the alert sounded in the station. "Headed out to a training exercise. It's an actual fire, but it's small. Ready to roll?" he asked.

"Of course." I hustled into the locker room and grabbed my gear. "What's the deal?" I asked as I fell into step beside Hudson and Parker a few minutes later.

"It's an old abandoned hunting cabin on the outskirts of town. Not sure how, but it caught fire. It's in an area with a lot of dead spruce from the spruce bark beetle kill. The town crew is in Anchorage today," Hudson explained.

I texted my parents on the way, letting them know I might be later than usual tonight. Hunting cabins were scattered all over Alaska. Many of them were actively in use, but there were also plenty that had been abandoned. This one might as well have been a pile of sticks. Unfortunately, someone left behind two rusted tanks of propane. Whatever set off the explosion had created a fast-burning fire.

We hustled that afternoon, setting a perimeter and getting most of the fire under control within a few hours. Part of the crew was going to stay back to monitor the fire for the night. We had to chase off a brown bear coming out of hibernation on the way out.

Bears were hungry during Alaska's spring. "Damn, he's hungry," I said to Parker, eyeing the bear's lean form.

"He's got his eye on them." Parker gestured toward a moose and a pair of calves in the distance.

"Aw, hell," I muttered.

"Looks like mama moose is headed straight toward town, which is probably for the best," Parker replied.

Aside from the fact that moose were plentiful in Alaska, the females often stayed close to towns when they had calves to protect. Bears were less likely to go where there were more people so they were safer. We guided the bear a few miles away from the fire and from town with two of our trucks.

When I got home a few hours later, I stopped at my parents' house first. My parents had a bedroom here for Dora. My dad liked to watch the news while Dora would curl up in the recliner with my parents' elderly mutt.

My dad waggled his brows as he looked up from his chair. "The news usually puts her to sleep."

I chuckled. Every so often, like tonight, I would look at Dora and marvel at how much she lived in my heart. I couldn't imagine life without her now. Which was remarkable, considering I hadn't even known she existed less than a year ago.

"Think she'll wake up when I bring her home?" I asked.

My dad shrugged. "Doubt it. She's a pretty sound sleeper."

My parents' dog thumped his little tail as he looked up at me. I bundled Dora into my arms. She didn't even blink. A few minutes later, I walked the short distance to my house through the trees. She woke up briefly when I tucked her in bed. We had a routine on the nights that my parents kept her past dinner when I was working. They got her changed into her pajamas and made sure she brushed her teeth. That made it easier for her. There was always the option to let her sleep at their place, but I preferred not to do that unless it was too late. I didn't know if that made sense, but I was trying to keep her routine in place as much as I could.

I ate some leftover pizza and plunked down on the couch after a shower. As soon as I had time to think, Casey slipped into my thoughts. Between the way it felt to be with her and learning more about her life, I didn't even know what to do with the way I felt.

Beyond replaying our kisses and the taste of her on my fingers time and again, I couldn't forget those few seconds where our eyes had locked at the end of our therapy appointment. It felt as if something flourished in the air between us, a sense of deep connection and intimacy.

I eyed my phone where it sat innocuously on the coffee table. I leaned forward and snagged it, quickly typing out a text to Casey.

Me: I'm not sure how to say this, but I appreciate you talking about what you've been going through.

After I hit send, I began to wonder if I should've said anything. Maybe it was strange because of how we started therapy, but it felt right that we were using our appointments to process what we were going through. It felt as if we were taking one step after another toward each other. What was happening between us also felt more real than any relationship I'd had before. It wasn't that Diane hadn't been important to me, but we'd been young and the way it ended had soured me on any nostalgia around it.

Before I could overthink too long, my phone vibrated, and I instantly glanced down.

Casey: I wasn't really planning to say all that today, but it just came out. You've been open about what you're dealing with, so I guess it's good we both are. Maybe it's awkward.

Without thinking, I tapped the screen to call her.

Casey answered immediately. "Hi!" Her voice was a little breathless.

"You don't need to worry about it being awkward," I said bluntly.

I could hear the shudder in her breath. The sound pierced my heart. I didn't know how the hell this had happened, but Casey had slipped into my heart so swiftly it was shocking.

"I appreciate that," she finally said. Another breath filtered through the line. "This is just all so unexpected. I'll be honest because I've already admitted it, I totally thought you were cute when you were coming to the café. When you were the unlucky guy in the waiting room and I dragged you into a therapy appointment, I don't know what I was thinking. I didn't know —" Her words sputtered abruptly. "The whole thing is ridiculous. I should've realized there's no way any therapist with any ethics would tell my parents whether or not I had a fiancé. I need to get over myself and tell my parents the truth and—"

When she paused to breathe, I cut in. "Take a breath, Casey. If we could all explain the things we did all the time and every-thing made sense, life would be pretty boring. I'm not a thera-pist, but I have a feeling we might end up telling Delaney the whole story. I think she might say that the situation around your sister's death is complicated and traumatic enough for you that it's hard for you to think clearly about it. It might seem logical that you needed someone to pretend like they were your fiancé just because of how much you're trying to hold back. Does that make sense?"

Casey was quiet for a few beats before her soft laugh filtered through the line. My heart twisted with piercing sweetness. I just wanted to hold her and protect her, to be her shelter when she needed it and the sunshine when she could use some brightness.

"It does," she said. "Every time I think about Callie, I feel a little panicked because I know I need to tell my parents what happened."

"I'll keep being your fake fiancé, but I hope I'm your real boyfriend."

She giggled. "I hope you are too, and I'll be your fake fiancée. I didn't expect this, but I actually like our therapy sessions."

"I actually like them too. I'm glad I was the random guy in the waiting room that day."

When she giggled again, heat sizzled through me. "I can't wait to see you Friday."

She let out a startled sound. "I can't wait to see you either."

I was just about to find a way to end this call when she added, "I hope I see you at the café before that. You need your coffee and Luna is making new donuts every day. She's expanding the variety."

"Casey, I don't really need coffee or donuts. Those are just an excuse for me to stop in and see you."

Chapter Fifteen

CASEY

"Leo said what?" Luna's eyes were wide.

Josie waggled her brows with her smile. "I have known for months that Leo is into you. All he needed was the opportunity."

I'd filled Josie and Luna in on the therapy situation, which they both thought was absolutely hysterical. Josie thought we should let our therapist know the whole story. I'd also told them what Leo said on the phone.

"You deserve this," Josie said after she took a big gulp of her coffee.

"You think?" I prompted.

Luna was checking on a batch of donuts and glanced over her shoulder. "Everybody deserves love."

"Luna speaks the truth." Josie nodded solemnly.

"I think calling it love is getting a little ahead of it. Leo said he uses coffee and donuts as an excuse to see me. That doesn't mean he's in love with me," I explained.

"Maybe you're not ready to admit it could be love, but I have a feeling," Luna said as she pulled a tray of donuts out of the oven.

"Let's do a tarot reading," Josie said.

Luna enjoyed doing tarot readings for us. For reasons I couldn't quite explain, it always made me a little nervous. I was afraid I would mess up what the universe was casting out for me, or I would miss the signs. Sometimes, life felt like a highway where I often took the wrong exit.

Before I could protest, Luna whipped out her tarot cards. Seeing as the café wasn't open yet, I couldn't find much of an excuse to dip out. Next thing I knew, she was explaining to me that the Knight of Cups card I'd drawn represented passion, romance, and emotions.

Leo came into the café later that morning, and Josie did a terrible job of hiding her glee.

"Josie!" I hissed when Leo turned to say something to Tate, her fiancé.

She winked, but blessedly, she toned it down a little. All the while, I found myself tongue-tied around Leo in front of other people. It wasn't supposed to be happening this way and I didn't even know what to do with the anticipation and fizzy joy I felt inside when I saw him.

Before I knew it, Friday rolled around. I thought I legit might have a meltdown over how ridiculously excited I was about our dinner date. The days flew by because the café was wildly busy.

"It's like this every spring," Janet explained. "There are tourists who think they can beat the rush. Instead, they start the rush."

I made so many variations of coffee drinks, my brain blurred. When I left that evening to walk to my apartment, a light drizzle started. I could hardly see the mountains through the mist and clouds blanketing the area.

The sarcastic, cynical corner of my brain decided now was the ideal time to make me question everything.

Just wait until Leo really gets to know you. This is just a honeymoon phase. Plus, don't forget you still have to figure out what to do about

Nathaniel. Maybe Leo is willing to be your fake fiancé, but at some point, reality will strike.

Thanks, anxiety.

"Shut up," I said out loud in my bathroom while I was toweling off after a shower. Much as I loved the smell of coffee and fresh baked goods, I didn't want to smell like them *all* the time.

I began to obsess about how I looked. "Maybe I should wear makeup," I said to my reflection. Followed with, "Oh, my God, get a fucking grip."

When my cell phone vibrated from where it sat on the bathroom counter, I nearly jumped out of my skin. Leo.

"Hey!" I practically yelped.

The sound of his low chuckle rumbled across my nerve endings and sent heat spinning in a swirl in my belly with tingles scattering throughout my body.

"I was wondering if I should pick you up," he said.

"Uh, sure," I finally said. I hadn't really thought that through. "Where are we going?"

"I thought we could go out to the new Fireweed Winery restaurant."

"Sounds perfect!"

Slow your roll. My brain rolled its eyes at me.

———

There was no chill to be had. I sat across from Leo at the restaurant, fiddling nervously with my napkin. My body felt like a pinball machine gone haywire with sparks and tingling nerves.

Just when I thought I'd forgotten how to have a regular conversation with anyone, much less Leo, our waitress arrived. She went over the specials and pointed out the favorites on the menu before telling us she'd check back soon.

"Casey?" Leo prompted.

I lifted my eyes to his. "Yeah?"

"You okay?"

I looked into his eyes and all my anxiety tumbled out in a long run-on sentence. "I'm nervous and I don't know what to think and it's raining and I wasn't sure if I should wear makeup and none of this is what I expected and I don't know what you're going to think and you're a single dad and I don't know how to talk to my parents about what happened with my sister and it's all just crazy and I'm overwhelmed." Thank God I needed to breathe because that was the only reason I managed to shut up.

When my words ran out, Leo was quiet before he reached across the table, clasping both of my hands in his strong, roughened grip. "It's okay, Casey."

"It is?"

His smile was warm. The anxiety spinning like an out-of-control wheel in my chest finally started to slow.

He nodded, squeezing my hands. "I'm nervous too."

I bit my lip, feeling sheepish. "So you don't think I'm crazy?"

"Absolutely not."

I let out a deep sigh. "Okay, well, that's good."

"You're beautiful. If you wear makeup, I'm sure you'll still be beautiful, but it doesn't matter. I just like you."

I wasn't sure whether to laugh or burst into happy tears. I blinked, considering that crying in the middle of a restaurant right now was the least chill thing I could do. I managed to take another breath. "I like you too."

When his eyes crinkled at the corners with his smile, my heart thumped along. It felt as if someone had flung the windows open, letting sunshine and a warm breeze into my heart. By the time we finished dinner, it was pouring rain outside.

I peered out the windows beside our table. With it being spring, the days were stretching longer. It was still light out, even though it was getting late.

I glanced across the table at Leo. "I'm still not used to these long days. I had to get used to short days in the winter and now it's the other way around."

When he grinned, my belly did a little flip. It was ridiculous how easily I reacted to him. It didn't take much—a smile, a crinkle at the corner of his eye, and my hormones were off to the races.

"You'll get used to it," he said.

"Long days or not, it's pouring out now," I pointed out.

While we'd been eating, clouds had thickened in the valley. The light drizzle had turned to heavy rain. He followed my gaze. "Let's go." He'd already taken care of the check and we'd gotten some chocolate raspberry mousse pie boxed up.

When we got to the entrance, I glanced up at him. "I didn't wear my raincoat."

He shrugged out of his jacket.

We dashed through the rain while I held my jacket above our heads. It helped a little, but not really. We were both laughing when we reached my truck. I held the door for Casey, and she scrambled inside before I jogged around to climb into the driver's side.

I tucked my wet jacket behind my seat. When I glanced over at Casey, her hair was wet and she was still laughing.

The desire that seemed to grow in force the more time I spent with her sizzled through me when our eyes collided.

"What?" she asked through her laughter.

"We're drenched." A laugh rustled in my throat.

She shrugged. "We are."

I loved that she thought it was funny. She seemed entirely unbothered.

"What now?" she prompted.

"Do you want to go to my place? I have a woodstove and we have that pie. It's spring, but it's chilly out with the rain. No expectations," I added.

She bit her lip before nodding. "Let's. I think dessert in front of a fire sounds perfect."

On the drive to my house, the rain came down harder. Casey

peered through the windows as my headlights angled toward my house.

"I live on my parents' property. This is where I grew up. You know Beck Steele, right?"

Casey snorted. "It's pretty impossible not to know Beck."

"So true," I returned. "Anyway, his parents live next door."

"Next door in Alaska is a little different than in a lot of places," Casey teased.

"Also true," I said dryly. "Anyway, there are two homes on the property. My parents moved back from Juneau after my grandparents passed away. Since they help out a lot with Dora, it's convenient. I honestly don't know what I would do without them."

"I imagine your life changed dramatically when Dora came into it," Casey said.

I parked and glanced over at her. "Most definitely. I can't imagine my life without her now."

"I think that's a good thing," Casey said softly.

I was relieved my outside lights were on a timer. With the pouring rain, a little visibility was a blessing.

"Do you want to use my jacket, or just go for it?"

"I'm going for it. Race you!" Casey flung the passenger door open and dashed into the rain.

I was laughing as I followed behind her. She made it to the top step first. She stopped in front of the door and waited for me.

"It's not locked." I reached around her and opened it.

I flicked on the lights and closed the door behind us. She stood in the entryway, curling her arms around her waist. Water dripped down around us onto the tiled floor.

She looked at my hands. "I think you won. You remembered to get the dessert."

I held the takeout box in my hands. "So what do I get for winning?" I teased.

When I saw her shiver, I hung up my wet jacket. "Just leave your shoes in here." I kicked mine off.

"I'm soaked," Casey pointed out. "I'm not sure this was such a good plan."

"You can shower," I offered.

"Are you sure?"

At my nod, she followed me out of the entryway into the living room.

The house was small, but perfect for me and Dora. There was a living room with a sunroom off to the side that offered a gorgeous view of the mountains and a field. We even had a small pond in the corner of the field. I'd turned the sunroom into a playroom for Dora. Beyond the living room was the kitchen and dining area with a table beside the windows, along with a small kitchen island. There was a bathroom with laundry off the kitchen.

To the opposite side of the living room was a hallway that led to three bedrooms. The main suite had a large bedroom and its own bathroom. There was also another bathroom with a shower in between the two smaller bedrooms. For a second, I contemplated showing Casey the shower by Dora's bedroom. I didn't, and I didn't really want to think about why.

I told myself now wasn't the time to take things further. I was a little unsettled inside with the sense of protectiveness Casey elicited. I wanted to bundle her up and hold her close until she was warm.

With a mental kick, I handed her a towel and a robe I never used and told her I'd wait in the living room. When she came out a few minutes later, her hair was still damp, but now her cheeks were flushed pink, and she was wearing my robe that trailed on the floor around her feet.

"Warm now?" I asked.

She nodded. "Your turn."

"Give me five," I said, as I walked past her. I raced through a hot shower and tossed on a dry T-shirt and sweatpants.

She had left her wet clothes in a tidy pile beside the hamper. I carried the hamper out to start a load of laundry. She was sitting on a stool in the kitchen when I returned.

"I feel silly," she announced.

"About what?"

Her pretty hazel eyes held mine and the pink flush on her cheeks deepened. "I'm wearing your robe."

When I met her eyes and saw her lips twitching as she tried to keep from smiling, a chuckle slipped out. "I started the laundry. You'll have dry clothes soon. Now, let me start a fire and we can eat that pie." I opened the refrigerator, peering inside. "Do you want anything to drink? I've got water, some beer, and cider from the winery."

"Ooh, let's heat up some of the cider. That would go perfect with the chocolate raspberry mousse."

I got a fire started, while Casey heated up the cider on the stove. A few minutes later, she came into the living room carrying two mugs. I tried not to let my eyes linger on the shadowed valley between her breasts. My robe was *way* too big for her. It trailed on the floor behind her, and she'd rolled the sleeves up. She sat down on the couch and tucked her feet under her knees before taking a swallow of cider and letting out a satisfied hum. "This is so good," she enthused.

"Everything from Fireweed Winery is good. Do they do the spiked hot cider where you're from?" I asked as I sat down on the couch with her.

The firelight flickering through the glass door on the woodstove glimmered on her auburn hair, illuminating streaks of gold.

She shook her head. "Not really. It's pretty hot there, so there aren't local apples. With the popularity of small breweries, you can certainly get it."

"Should we try that pie?"

Her eyes lit up as she nodded. A few minutes later, I realized my mistake. Watching Casey's lips close around the fork as she let out a moan with every single bite left me tied up in knots.

After another bite, she set her fork down, announcing, "I can't eat anymore."

The pie was good, but, in all honesty, I was hardly paying attention. Her presence had taken over my senses. I wanted to tug Casey into my lap and unwrap her like a present.

I set my plate down. When I looked over, her eyes held mine.

There was maybe a foot separating us on the couch and she shifted, shimmying closer to me. "You know, it's raining."

"I know." My voice was ragged on the edges.

"What are we doing?" she whispered.

I tried to take a breath, but my lungs felt constrained. My body was wound tight with energy, electricity racing in a circuit.

I shifted on the couch to face her more fully. "I don't know. I think we've established that we might both want something more, but I don't want to rush you."

Casey's eyes skated over my face. She was quiet for a beat before she leaned over and lifted her mug of cider to take a swallow. When her tongue darted out to swipe across her bottom lip, that electricity sizzled straight to my cock. I forced myself to rein it in, to keep control, not to reach for her and pull her into my lap.

She put her mug back on the coffee table. "You're not rushing me. We're here. It's raining and I don't want to leave."

She leaned close, just enough for me to slide my arm around her waist. She pressed a kiss in the divot at the base of my throat. Her touch was like a drop of liquid fire on my skin, heat radiating outward. When she lifted her head, she whispered, "Am I rushing you?"

"No," I said flatly.

She shimmied closer. Just before her lips met mine, I checked her, holding her still with a palm on her chest. Her skin was warm. "Tell me, and we'll stop at any point. Okay?"

She blinked and nodded. "I didn't want to stop the other night. I don't know what this is, but we have to see it through."

My pulse was rampaging out of control, and I barely had a grip on my control. "Right there with you, sweetheart, but what I said still stands."

"The same goes for you," she whispered. "Just to make sure that's clear."

A strangled laugh escaped.

"What?" she asked.

"I want it all with you."

Her lips curled at the corners, her smile sensual and teasing. "We're on the same page then. Now, can I kiss you?"

Chapter Seventeen

LEO

... can I kiss you?

With Casey's eyes burning into mine, my answer was to slide my hand around her nape, my fingers tangling in her hair as I brought my mouth to hers, diving into the warm sweetness. She made this startled little whimper in her throat. In a matter of seconds, our kiss exploded in a tangle of lips and tongues. She moved closer and straddled me. I slid my hands up her legs. It didn't help matters at all that I knew she was naked underneath this robe.

When I felt the press of her curves against me, I broke away, sucking in deep gulps of air. She shimmied her hips, rocking over the ridge of my arousal.

"Casey," I bit out. "We need to slow down. I don't want to ruin this for you."

Casey's eyes held mine. "That's impossible."

With her a bundle of lush curves in my lap, her robe falling open, and her skin flushed a deep shade of pink, my mind was hazed with fiery need. I closed the small distance between us and claimed her mouth again. A sizzle of gratification burned through me at how quickly she opened to me.

I blazed a trail of kisses down the side of her neck, loving it as I felt her tremble, and goosebumps rise on her skin. I slid my hands down over her shoulders, she straightened a little, rolling her shoulders until the robe fell in a rumple around her waist.

My breath hissed through my teeth as I took the moment to soak in the sight of her bare before me. Her breasts were plump and flushed pink. I cupped both of them, teasing my thumbs over her ruched nipples. She bit her lip, letting out a little whimper.

My cock was swollen near to the point of pain and every little motion she made sent blood arrowing straight to it. "Fuck me," I muttered through gritted teeth.

"That's the whole point," she teased, her voice sultry and throaty.

I chuckled before dipping my head and sucking a nipple into my mouth. She cried out, her fingers spearing my hair. I teased both nipples before lifting my head.

We stared at each other through several kicks of my heart. I palmed her cheek, dragging my thumb in a slow stroke across her bottom lip. Her tongue darted out, nipping lightly.

"Tell me what you want," I rasped.

She reached between us as she shimmied back slightly on my lap, dragging her palm over my swollen length. "This," she said bluntly.

It was a fucking miracle I didn't come right there. "All yours," I choked out.

Over the following fiery hot seconds, she moved back swiftly, shoving my sweatpants down around my hips. Since I'd just showered, I didn't even have boxers on and my cock sprang free. She curled her palm around it, her eyes on mine when she slid her thumb over the drop of cum rolling out the tip. I could barely breathe, much less think.

In another few seconds, she was kneeling before me, her eyes on mine as she dragged her tongue along the side of my cock murmuring, "Is this okay?"

I didn't even remember if I managed to form a single word. My head fell back against the couch when her lips closed around my crown and she sucked me into the warm sweetness of her mouth. I clung to my control, one hand tangling in her hair and the other gripping the edge of the couch.

She teased, drawing back and lazily circling her tongue around the crown before sucking me deep, again and again. I could feel my release threatening and choked out her name. She leaned back, releasing me with a little pop. I couldn't hold back any longer and my release spurted out over her hand. She slid her palm up my length once again, her eyes on me.

Moments later, I managed to stand and follow her into the kitchen. She washed her hands and turned to face me.

I reached for her hand. "Your turn, sweetheart."

Chapter Eighteen

CASEY

It felt as if lava was running through my veins, the heat sizzling through me. As I stood there before Leo with my robe fallen open, his eyes swept up and down.

When he said, "Your turn, sweetheart," I thought my knees might give out.

He closed the distance between us and dipped his head, blazing kisses down my neck and between my breasts before he caught a nipple in his mouth and gave it a sharp suck. The piercing pleasure arrowed to the core of me. My arousal was slick on the insides of my thighs.

All I could do was try to breathe. My mind was a haze of pure want. He muttered something before spinning away. For a moment, I was confused until he returned to the kitchen, tearing open a condom as he walked.

The next few moments were a blur. On shaky knees, I followed him back into the living room. He rolled the condom on, his eyes locked to mine. "Come back here to my lap, sweetheart."

I'd never cared about any man using an endearment for me, but the way Leo said "sweetheart" snagged along the ragged edge of my heart. In the burning hazy moments that followed, I straddled him again, his dark blue gaze holding mine as he notched his thick crown at my entrance. I sank down over him, sheathing him inside me.

I was trembling all over, chasing my release instantly. I cried out at the feeling of his thick length stretching and filling me completely. Somewhere along the way, my robe had been tossed to the floor with his shirt and sweatpants. The crinkly feel of the dark hair on his chest brushed against my skin, the sensation spinning like fire into all the others shivering through me.

I felt liquid, my mind solely focused on the sharp pleasure tightening inside of me as we rocked together. Our kiss was messy, sensual, and slow.

He leaned his head back, whispering, "Come for me, sweetheart."

I felt the press of his fingers on one hip as he controlled our tempo. He slipped his other hand between us, teasing my swollen clit, giving me just enough pressure to topple me over. My releasee finally crested with wave after wave of pleasure rolling through me as I cried out, shocked to hear myself panting his name.

His teeth grazed the side of my neck before he captured my cries with a kiss. He thrust once more to fill me completely. I felt the shudder of his release as he jerked inside of me. I finally collapsed against him, his arms holding me tight as we trembled together.

I had no idea how much time passed before the storm of my climax receded. I gradually cataloged sensations. His muscled chest pressed against my softness, his hand sliding up and down my back in lazy strokes, his other arm around my waist as he held me close. My head tucked into the curve of his neck, breathing in his scent, a little woodsy and crisp, and my breath gusting across his collarbone.

I felt the rumble of his voice against my ear on the side of his neck. "How are you?"

His question made me giggle. I lifted my head, meeting his eyes. "Amazing," I answered.

His lips kicked up in a smile. "Same."

His hand slid up my back, his fingers sifting through the ends of my hair. His gaze sobered as he studied me. "That was more than I expected."

A startling sense of intimacy kept flourishing between us. When it came to Leo, my emotions felt like flowers bursting through barren ground in my heart. It was almost more than I knew how to take. I swallowed through the sudden thickness in my throat as I nodded. "It was," I managed to whisper.

Leo was solicitous over the next few minutes as we disentangled ourselves. He helped me back into his robe and went to switch the laundry into the dryer.

When he returned to the living room, he asked, "Do you want to stay?"

Chapter Nineteen

CASEY

Do you want to stay?

At Leo's question, I nodded so fast I almost gave myself whiplash. The weekend passed in a blur.

The next day, he asked if I wanted to go for a hike. I loved trying anything new in Alaska, so I was happy to go along. After stopping by my apartment and making sure I had a decent pair of hiking boots and a jacket, we set out on a crisp spring morning. He drove us out to an old ski lodge under renovation. Since the snow was melting on the slopes, we hiked up to the top. I spun in a circle, letting out a whoop at the three-hundred-and-sixty-degree view.

Back at his house after the sun had set and darkness fell again, I didn't want to go home. I wanted another night with him. The next morning, he took me on a drive out to a glacial lake. Until you saw the clear blue waters of a glacial lake tucked in the mountains, it was difficult to believe how blue and clear the water could be.

"When does Dora come home?" I asked that afternoon.

"Monday."

I stayed with Leo for one more night. In the darkness, after we fell asleep, after he had once again taken my body on a journey of pure pleasure, my eyes blinked open. I was asleep on my back, and Leo was curled up on his side with his big, warm palm resting on my belly. One of my calves was tucked against his and I could feel the crinkly feel of the hair on his legs when I moved slightly. I rolled my head to the side to see the clock on the nightstand. It read five a.m., the numbers glowing in the darkness.

I was aroused, my body thrumming with awareness and need. The cotton sheet abraded against the tight peaks of my nipples. I could feel the slick wetness at the apex of my thighs. I took a little breath as my pulse began to skitter when his palm moved slightly. The calloused surface of his palm sent sparks scattering over my skin. I sensed when he came awake, a humming tension emanating from his body.

"Casey," his voice was low and rumbly, almost a little crushed on the edges from sleep.

"Yeah?" I whispered in the darkness.

When he moved, I felt the brush of his arousal, the skin hot and velvety soft against my hip. I had to bite my lip to keep from moaning. I was a little shocked at my responsiveness to Leo. My body felt ready to go off whenever he was near. I was used to being more perfunctory about sex. I wouldn't go so far as to say all the sex I'd had was bad, but it was mediocre. With Leo, sex was something else altogether. My physical attraction to him was intense. Just lying here in the darkness with the sheets over me and his palm on my belly, I could feel my clit throbbing. I shifted my legs restlessly. I couldn't help it. I was so wet the insides of my thighs were damp from my arousal.

"I was going to ask if you're awake, but that seems a little silly," he said before moving closer, sliding his palm up my belly to my breasts.

I arched into his touch, shamelessly whispering, "Leo..."

"What do you want, sweetheart?" He lazily traced his thumb over one nipple and then the other.

I shifted my legs again. He rocked his hips against my side, and I felt a little smear of moisture there. That was another thing about this. Knowing how turned on he was fed into my desire, amping it higher and higher.

I bit my lip to keep from moaning when he slid his hand down over my belly. He leaned over and pushed the sheet down to press hot kisses in the valley between my breasts.

He repeated his question, his lips shaping the words on my skin. "What do you want, sweetheart?"

"You," I gasped, this time not hesitating to whimper when his mouth closed over a nipple and he gave it a hard suck. The sensation went straight down, and my pussy clenched, as I shifted my hips restlessly.

I let my knees fall apart when he teased his fingers into my dripping folds. "Oh, Casey," he murmured against my belly.

I whimpered again, rocking my hips up when he lightly dipped a finger down, sliding it through the wetness and teasing a lazy circle around my throbbing clit. He teased me with glanced touches until I was crying out and begging. He tossed the sheets aside, dropping hot kisses on my belly and pushing my knees apart.

"Look at me," he ordered.

I was hot and panting, and I looked down to see his face right above my sex, his eyes glittering in the light cast from the bathroom. He sank two fingers inside of me and my hips rocked up roughly.

Everything blurred. I felt liquid inside and out when he brought his mouth to my sex and my head fell back. He fucked me with his fingers and his mouth, teasing me until I was begging and crying. Finally, *finally*, he sank his two fingers in deeply and sucked on my clit, and my climax burst through me. I felt as if I were flying apart.

My body was still trembling from the aftershocks when he

rose above me, swiftly rolling a condom on. While I was still shuddering, he filled me in a deep thrust. I cried out at the intense stretch. One orgasm rolled into the next.

With his weight over me and his hands holding mine above my head, his eyes bored into mine. He fucked me slow and hard and deep. His body shivered when he thrust inside me once more. He swiftly rolled us over moments later, and I rested against him and tried to breathe.

His palm smoothed up my back, lazily sifting his fingers through my hair. "I'm going to miss you," he whispered gruffly.

My heart felt cleaved wide open, soft, and vulnerable, as every beat echoed through my body. "I'm going to miss you too."

Chapter Twenty

CASEY

That morning, I was due to leave early to go into the café. It was still dark when Leo got up with me. "I can drive you in," he offered.

Fresh from a shower, my hair was damp and my skin still warm. "You don't have to."

His brows arched up, his lips twitching at the corners.

"Oh, I don't have my car." I smiled sheepishly.

He grinned. "You could walk."

I bit my lip to keep from laughing. "I appreciate the ride."

His gaze sobered. "What is this to you?"

I cleared my throat, my pulse starting to kick up its pace and anxiety spinning in my belly. Emotion crested inside of me.

Before I could answer, he reached for my hand. "I don't know where this is going, but it's important to me. You know I have a lot going on with Dora, but this is real for me."

Tears stung my eyes, and I blinked them away quickly. My heart felt as if it were clapping inside my chest. "It's real for me too, but what does that mean?"

"I think it means if we both feel this way, we keep seeing each other. We could discuss it with Delaney and tell her the whole story," he said, his lips twisting to the side with a half-smile.

"Let's tell her. We might as well."

His eyes held mine, and heat started to suffuse me while my belly felt tingly. "When I see you at the café, do I pretend we're friends, or something else?"

Joy, anticipation, and anxiety were bubbling over inside me. "Something else."

Maybe I didn't even know what I meant by that, but I didn't want to sneak around with Leo.

Chapter Twenty-One

CASEY

One month later

Luna smiled as she studied the tarot card I'd just pulled. "Just what I would expect," she said, nodding sagely as if it made perfect sense.

I adored Luna, but I tended to feel a little flustered by how down-to-earth and simultaneously woo-woo she was. She really believed this tarot stuff, while I was skeptical of it. Of course, I was generally skeptical about life.

"Why would you expect this?" I asked, eyeing the too-on-the-nose Lovers card.

"Because I think you're falling in love." She was completely serious. I had just taken a sip of coffee and nearly choked, almost spitting it out on the table in front of us.

Josie was standing beside me, her hip resting against the stainless-steel table. "I agree."

"What?!" I sputtered.

Josie patted me on the back as if I were a small child. "Oh, sugar. As you would say, bless your heart. Leo comes in every day you're working. He's gaga over you. He's also nice."

"He's also totally hot," Luna offered helpfully. "Not my type, but I have eyes."

My face was on fire as I looked between my friends. I couldn't imagine being in love, but I was afraid they might be right. It was really difficult for me to believe that a guy like Leo would be into me.

I kept telling myself to just take it one day at a time and live in the moment and all those trite phrases. I was trying to stay calm, but my internal state was so heightened that it felt impossible.

"You've been talking with your therapist about it. Didn't you say last week that she feels like you could meet Dora and his parents? They know about you anyway," Josie said.

"They do?" I yelped.

Josie waggled her brows. "Of course they do! In case you didn't notice, this is a small town. I know Leo's parents. His mom asked me about you, and I told her you were awesome."

A sense of panic spun in my chest. Although this started out teasing, Josie's gaze sobered. "Hey, hey, it's okay. Just remember, you can take things one day at a time."

I was busy telling myself that later that day when I walked up the stairs to my apartment and my phone chimed with an incoming text. When I glanced down and saw Nathaniel's name flash on the screen, that sense of panic felt like a tsunami inside of me.

Nathaniel: Why the hell are you talking to the police?

My thoughts spiraled. Seeing as I hadn't talked to the police, I had zero clue why he thought I had.

Chapter Twenty-Two

LEO

Dora stared at me, hands on her hips with her eyes narrowed. If you had tried to tell me before I was the full-time parent of a six-year-old that they could boss you around, I wouldn't have believed it. I found it harder to hold my ground with Dora than with full-grown men who were bigger than me.

"Dora," I began, clearing my throat. "I don't know if we can have a dog."

She'd gotten it into her head that we needed a pet.

"Why not?" She blinked up at me.

Holy fucking hell. How am I supposed to let her down?

My reasoning behind the dog was that I could be gone for a few weeks at a time when I got called out to fires. My parents made it possible for me to have Dora and keep my job. Considering that this situation had happened on the fly for me, I'd had to just roll with it. I didn't think I should add the responsibility of a dog to my parents, seeing as they already had an elderly one to care for.

Of course, there was Casey. I wanted to bring Casey more fully into my life. I was ready for her to meet Dora. We'd planned for it to happen this coming weekend at my parents' house. I knew they would adore her. Who wouldn't? She was amazing.

"Dad?" Dora prompted, bringing my thoughts back to the moment.

"What about a cat?" I asked, thinking I could handle a cat.

"Yes!" Dora practically shouted.

"Yes, what?"

"I want a cat."

"Okay, well—"

Before I could finish, Dora beamed. "Let's go today!" She turned and raced down the hallway to her bedroom, coming back with her shoes and the small plastic bucket she was referring to as her purse.

"Where are we going?" I asked.

"The pet place. Tiffany told me about it," my daughter said, looking at me as if I was slow.

"Ohhhh." I finally connected the dots.

"Did you meet Tiffany with Grammy?" I asked as Dora put her shoes on.

She'd just learned to tie them last week. The amount of pride I felt at the fact she could do this seemed wildly out of proportion to the task, but I figured that was part of being a dad. Everything she learned to do herself made me so proud.

She was sitting on this little stool my dad had built for her. He'd made it out of a tree trunk, and it was the right height for her. She would get too tall for it, but she loved it. My dad promised to make her a new one when she needed it. She was very focused on her task and stuck her feet out to study the ties before she finally answered my question. "I met Tiffany with Grammy and she said there's a place where they keep all of the pets who need a home and that I should ask you about it."

I chuckled. "Of course she did."

Wes, a fellow hotshot firefighter and friend, helped his mom with the local animal rescue program. Tiffany, his wife, also helped out and managed the local vet clinic. She was constantly trying to find people to take animals from the program.

"Here's the deal," I began as I looked down at Dora. She put this wallet my mom had gotten her into her bucket. "We'll go look, but we have to wait to pick up the cat until this weekend if we find one because we need to get some things for it."

Dora bounced up and down, her bucket swinging in her hand. "Okay!"

As I drove into town a few minutes later, I wanted to stop and see Casey at Firehouse Café, but with Dora with me, I hesitated. We had a plan. We'd gone over it with our therapist. If I stopped by with Dora now, she'd meet Casey and have a million questions when Casey later showed up for dinner.

When we arrived at the rescue program, Wes was there with Tiffany. Tiffany smiled down at Dora. "Hey, girl!"

When Tiffany met my gaze, I prompted, "Cat?"

She grinned. "No dog?"

"Tiffany, you know that having a dog isn't the greatest option for a hotshot firefighter, especially one who's a single dad," I explained, keeping my voice low. Dora had already hurried over to look at the photos of cats eligible for adoption.

"Excellent point," Wes chimed in, narrowing his eyes at Tiffany. "Not to mention, we usually have more cats than dogs," he added dryly.

Tiffany laughed as Wes curled his arm around her waist and gave her a quick squeeze before crossing over to open the doorway into the back. "Let's go meet the cats."

It took Dora a mere five minutes to declare that we needed to adopt them all, but when I explain that wasn't an option, she spun in a circle before sitting down beside two cats.

Wes glanced at me. "That's a bonded pair," he said under his breath. "Their owner passed away."

"How old are they?" I asked.

"Conveniently, we have their vet records. They're only two years old and already litterbox trained."

Wes glanced over at Dora who had both cats in her lap now. "When you are out dealing with a fire, the cats won't be lonely," Wes pointed out with a brow waggle.

Next thing I knew, I had agreed to adopt a pair of cats. I got a big hug from Tiffany and Dora. I was prepared for Dora to beg for us to take them home today, but she was so excited that she didn't care she had to wait.

It was Thursday, so we just had to make it to Saturday. We had dinner tomorrow with my parents, Dora, and Casey. My mom had already planned for a slumber party and movie night with Dora after dinner. I figured we'd get the cats together on Saturday. Now that I had agreed to this, I might as well take full advantage and have it be an activity with Casey that might be bonding for Dora. Our therapist had suggested coming up with something and this seemed perfect.

As we drove away, I marveled, as I did pretty much daily, at how much I had absorbed Dora into my life. Much as I wanted to see Casey every single night, I knew we weren't in that place yet, not when it came to Dora. I didn't mind waiting because Dora was my priority.

"Daddy?" Dora piped up from the back where she was buckled into her car seat.

When she called me "Daddy", I thought my heart might split open from the combination of piercing joy sliced through with pain. I loved it and it also hurt that I'd missed so many years with her. For a split second, I would be angry with Diane but then I'd remember it didn't matter anymore because Diane was gone.

I caught Dora's eyes in the rearview mirror. "What's up?"

"Thank you," she said in a singsong voice.

"For what?"

"For letting us adopt two cats. I know you're probably worried about it."

"Why would I be worried?"

"Because now you'll have more than me to take care of."

I caught her eyes in the rearview mirror. "Dora, I love taking care of you. Please don't ever worry about that. Two cats will be easy. We just have to get a few things so we can take care of them properly."

She bounced her feet against the bottom of her car seat. "You like to do things properly. Like you take care of me properly."

I smiled as I caught her eyes again in the rearview mirror before looking back at the road. "I try. I haven't had a cat since I was a little boy. We used to have one."

"You did?" The surprise in her voice drew a chuckle.

Chapter Twenty-Three

LEO

"Grammy says you're bringing a friend to dinner."

I looked over at Dora. "I am. Is that okay?"

My mom was so happy I was dating someone that she'd asked all around town about Casey. She'd concluded from her "reliable sources" that Casey was a good person and we should get married.

Dora blinked with her nod. "Yes. Is she your girlfriend?"

"She is," I said slowly.

"How come I haven't met her yet?"

God help me. I'd quickly learned the questions from children were relentless.

"Well, you're my priority, Dora. I wanted to wait until it felt like a good time for you to meet her." I was winging it here, but I figured the truth was my only safe option.

"Well, I think you should get married."

"What?" I sputtered. "You do?"

Dora nodded solemnly as she reached for her bucket purse. "Then, I can have a mommy again."

And now, I was floundering. I never quite knew how to talk about Dora's mom with her. I cleared my throat. "You had a mommy, she's just not here anymore."

"I know. She died." My daughter's matter-of-fact tone twisted my heart. "I'll always miss her, but I would like a mommy here."

My throat started to feel tight. She looked so earnest. "I understand that. I don't know if that will happen, but you have me, and Gramps and Grammy."

Chapter Twenty-Four

CASEY

My footsteps echoed in the hallway where I was pacing and peering out the window that faced the parking lot, hoping to see when Leo arrived. I was the cliché of a hot mess. I was meeting Dora, and I was so anxious about what this meant. I felt like I was going to jump out of my skin with restlessness and my pulse was a driving drumbeat echoing through me.

When I heard the sound of tires on gravel and glanced out to see Leo's truck, I dashed down the stairs, meeting him at the door just as he was reaching to open it. "Hi!" I all but yelped.

He smiled slowly. "Hey. You doing okay?"

I stepped out, making sure the door locked behind me. "Just a little nervous."

Leo took a step closer, leaning down to give me a kiss. His warmth and strong presence felt like a force field, soothing me a little.

When he straightened, his smile was a little sheepish. "I'm a little nervous too," he offered. "It'll be okay."

"What if it's not?" I fretted.

I could feel the low rumble of his chuckle where my palm had landed on his chest. His eyes were warm. "Dora's friendly.

And, so are you." He stepped back, reaching for my hand as it fell away from his chest.

A short while later, we were there. Martha and George were kind and easygoing. They'd welcomed me warmly. The tension and anxiety that had been churning up a storm inside had finally started to ease. Dora was, of course, adorable and sweet. She hadn't seemed all that interested in me after the first few minutes. She'd shown me a project she was working on that involved building a model volcano with her grandfather. She explained that she was trying to model it realistically after Mount Iliamna, which was visible from Anchorage.

After dinner, Dora went to work on her volcano while we stayed at the table. Leo's mother didn't try to hide her curiosity. "So, what do you think of Alaska?" she asked after we had finished eating and she'd served us coffee.

"It's absolutely beautiful." Safe answer, I thought.

"It certainly is. So, what brought you here?"

My mind silently tumbled through the whole answer, which was that I had been gallivanting all over the country, traveling to try to escape the pain from the loss of my sister. I never wanted to go back home even though I missed it because then I would have to stare down the pain and the secrets I was keeping. That was *way* more complicated than the partial truth.

"Alaska was a bucket list place for me. I always wanted to visit the last frontier and see the wilderness. It's so different from where I grew up," I explained.

Martha nodded along, her smile warm. "Alaska is full of transplants. It sounds like you might be staying?" Her voice lilted up in question.

Leo's hand was on my knee under the table and he squeezed gently. He'd warned me his mom was all in with the marriage plan.

"That's the plan for now. I'm enjoying working at the café. While that may not be a forever job, I sure love it."

Leo's father came walking in from where he and Dora were

working on her volcano project, and he heard the tail end of my comment. "Firehouse Café has the best coffee in Alaska and maybe even the country," he teased.

"It *is* very good." I grinned.

"Dora would love the group to come take a look," he said as he waggled his brows.

We all followed him into a room off the side of the living room area. The project was on a large table. Dora was waiting for us, wearing an apron with stars scattered all over it.

"Ta-da!" She swept her arms toward the table.

Dora's father had a photograph of Mount Iliamna propped up against the wall beside the table.

We collectively enthused over the project. Dora was so proud when Leo high-fived her and picked her up to spin her in a circle. As I watched them, my heart squeezed tight. Although I knew, chronologically-speaking, that their relationship was pretty new, you could literally feel the love Leo felt for her.

When Dora looked over at me, I lifted my hand and she slapped her small palm against mine. "That looks just like Mount Iliamna. Alaska has many volcanoes to choose from. We're in the ring of fire," I explained.

"What's that?" Dora asked as Leo set her back on the floor.

"It's a partial circle of volcanoes in the ocean near here," I replied.

"Wow! That's so cool you know that." Her eyes sparkled as she smiled up at me.

"I read about Alaska before I moved here."

A little while later, it was time for Dora and her grandmother to watch Dora's favorite science show. She hugged Leo good night and offered me a hug as well. After she scampered down the hallway to the TV room, Martha glanced over at me. "That went very well. It was lovely to meet you. Now, go and have a good night."

After we walked into his house a few minutes later, I caught his eyes. "I didn't consider feeling embarrassed about coming over here to stay with you."

He chuckled. "We're adults."

"Easy for you to say, they're your parents." My cheeks got hot just thinking about it.

"I told them I was taking you home," he added.

I rolled my eyes. "Leo, I think they know better."

He waggled his brows and pulled me in for a kiss. Once again, I let myself get swept up in the fire he kindled inside of me.

Chapter Twenty-Five

CASEY

"Did you suspect?" I pressed, laughing a little when our therapist shrugged.

"I knew I was missing some information that was significant, but I wasn't sure what that was. When couples come to see me for therapy, I'm not assessing just two individuals, but also the dynamic between them. I sensed a little discomfort and uncertainty between you two. But anybody can feel like that in a therapy appointment. I also sensed that you were holding something back. I've learned not to make assumptions and to wait because usually, the story comes out. I didn't know if it was something big or small. I like this reason. It's amusing. In the big scheme of things, as strange as this might sound, there are lies that I would be a lot more concerned about than this one. I love that you were both crushing on each other and that you're a real couple now. You've used your time here in a productive way. So..." She sobered, her gaze bouncing between us. "I don't just mean for the relationship issues."

Before I knew it, tears splashed onto my cheeks, and Leo handed me a tissue.

"You've both been dealing with a lot. We never know what

someone is actually going through, and I'm glad you're able to talk about it here," Delaney said softly.

I managed to collect myself, sniffling as I said, "I didn't mean to lose it like that. It feels like everything is big right now. I met Dora." I flung my hands in the air in emphasis.

"How do you feel like it went?" she asked.

"Good, I think?" I glanced at Leo.

He cast me an encouraging smile. "I thought it went well. Dora liked Casey. My parents were great. Dora got to show off the volcano model she's building with my dad. My mom and Dora did their weekly TV night and slumber party. Like you suggested, we stuck to what we'd usually do that night and just added Casey to the mix." He paused and ran a hand through his hair, one of his nervous gestures. "Dora told me before she met Casey that she wanted a new mommy, and now she thinks Casey could be that." His eyes met mine, uncertainty flickering there.

"That's understandable for her. She's looking for stability," Delaney said.

"I know, I just—" Leo leaned forward, running both hands through his hair and looking as flustered as I felt.

Delaney leaned forward, her gaze calm. "Leo, you could've had a girlfriend before you even found out about Dora, you could've been married. You had no idea Dora existed. It's okay to have a relationship when you have a child. I absolutely support you taking it slow because of everything Dora has been through. From what I'm hearing from you, Dora is adjusting well, all things considered. The environment you have created for her sounds more stable than what she had before. That isn't to be hurtful toward her mother, but it's more of a practical understanding."

"Okay, okay." Leo let out a deep sigh. "I just don't want to screw this up."

"You're doing as well as you can and that's all any parent can do. I love that you're bringing your questions here and that you

and Casey are talking on your own. Just take it one step at a
time. What do you think, Casey?"

Chapter Twenty-Six

LEO

It felt like time was flying by, as if I was on a high-speed train, watching the scenery in a blur. In the midst of it, our crew got called out to a fire. The interior of Alaska was largely unsettled. There were some Alaska Native villages scattered within the wilderness, along with some remote outdoor resorts and hunting cabins. This roaring wildfire was visible from the road that cut through the central part of the state and led up toward the Arctic Circle.

Dora squeezed me hard before I left. She said she'd miss me, but my parents had plenty of things planned for her and she was excited for all of it. I stopped by Firehouse Café to see Casey before I left. We had time for a quick, fierce kiss in the back before I had to go. My heart ached when I left.

I was going to miss her. Ever since our appointment the other day and her meeting Dora, we had stuck to the plan of one night a week together. And now, I wouldn't even have that. Our hotshot crew would likely be out for a week or more.

I couldn't quite pin it down, but I sensed Casey was worrying about something else and holding back. I would have to wonder until I returned.

Chapter Twenty-Seven

CASEY

I zipped through making coffees for a rush of customers. Janet and I had settled into a good rhythm of working together. She usually did a lot of the chitchatting and handling the register and food. She insisted I was much faster than her with the espresso machine. I tended to agree, but I knew it was mostly because she was starting to get arthritis in her hands. Every time I thought about that, it made my heart hurt a little bit.

Maybe I had only lived in Willow Brook for a little while, but I adored Janet. She had welcomed me into this town so warmly. I just wanted everything to be good for her, for always. I didn't want her to have arthritis.

I glanced around, moving on auto-pilot and prepping to make another drink when Janet tapped me on the shoulder. "What?" My ponytail whipped around as I turned to look at her.

"Hon, no more customers. You can breathe now." She glanced at the clock on the wall, shaking her head as she chuckled. "We have not had a break for two hours straight. Why don't you head in the back and sit down?"

Resting my hands on my hips, I shook my head. "I'm not taking a break unless you take a break."

Josie came through from the back. "How about you both

take a break?" She tied an apron around her waist. "I'm here for the afternoon."

Janet grinned when Josie clasped her by the shoulders and aimed her toward the swinging door into the back. "Go sit in the break room." She glanced my way, narrowing her eyes. "Make sure she actually sits down, okay?"

"Yes, ma'am!" I teased.

As we were walking through the door, Josie called, "Should I bring you two some coffee?"

"Yes, please!" Janet tossed over her shoulder.

Janet went to the restroom, and I stepped into the small break room at the back corner of the kitchen. It was tiny, but it had all the things, including a small round table, a refrigerator, and its own coffee machine, which was completely redundant. There were cubbies for staff to tuck jackets and things. I reached into the cubby and fished out my phone, just to check it.

When I saw there was a voicemail, I tapped the speaker and began to play it. My mouth dropped open as I listened.

Ms. Houston, this is Officer Blankenship from the sheriff's department in Carteret County in North Carolina. I'm calling to find out if you would be willing to talk to me. Nathaniel Smith is under investigation and we think you might have information that could be helpful to our case. If you could please call me back as soon as possible, I would appreciate it.

Janet arrived in the break room with Josie on her heels. Josie thrust two mugs at us, saying, "Fill me in later. I have to deal with customers."

Janet eyed me, pulling a chair out and practically shoving me into it. "Why do you look so scared?" she asked as she sat down across from me.

Janet knew the outlines of what happened to my sister, but I'd kept the details vague. Not because I didn't trust her, but because it hurt to talk about. I quickly filled her in, ending with, "And now, the police are investigating him. What should I do?"

"Call him back!" She slapped her palm on the table for emphasis.

"Right now?"

Janet rolled her eyes. "ASAP. I know you've been ordered to make sure I stay in the break room, but if you'd like some privacy, it's all yours," she added.

"I could use the moral support." Before I could chicken out, I called the police officer back.

Fully expecting to get his voicemail, I was startled when he answered. "Officer Blankenship here. Thank you for calling me back so quickly, Casey."

Janet patted my elbow when I cleared my throat nervously. "Of course," I replied. "I'm not sure how I can help you, but you can ask me anything."

"I'll try to keep it brief. Nathaniel Smith is a suspect in an investigation regarding another ketamine-related death. In the interviews our team has conducted, your sister has come up more than once. It appears he was the primary dealer for your sister and that they were dating. I don't know how much you know about this, but ketamine is a national problem. Dealers strengthen their products to increase the likelihood that people will become addicted. Those addictions provide a long-term source of income for dealers. While they may not be actively trying to kill the people they're selling to, more and more people are dying as a result. We believe that's what happened to your sister."

I took an uneasy breath, swallowing through the anxiety, grief, and anger that felt strangling inside my throat.

"Casey?" the police officer prompted.

"I'm here," I said, my voice strained. "That's what I think happened to my sister. I didn't know what to do because I didn't know how to prove it. I can confirm Nathaniel was often at her apartment, including the night she died." I paused, blinking back the tears stinging my eyes. "Nathaniel is a family friend. His parents are close to mine. I don't want you to think I want to protect him. I just didn't know how to go about proving what I suspected."

"You're not the first person who's shared these same concerns. These things are hard to prove. If it was just a one-off event, we might not even start digging. At this point, there are four deaths connected to Nathaniel."

"Oh, wow," I breathed. I sagged in my chair as the enormity of the situation struck me.

I accepted that my sister was responsible for her own actions. I knew how her substance abuse problem developed. I knew she had become desperate. I intellectually understood all of it. The anger I felt toward anyone who traded in those drugs felt suffocating if I thought about it.

"So, what happens now?" I finally asked.

"We have a strong case. At this point, our team is interviewing everyone we can to corroborate what we already know."

"Have I been able to provide anything helpful?"

"Absolutely. It may not feel like it to you, but you're able to confirm the whereabouts of Nathaniel at your sister's apartment, including on the night that she died. You're also able to confirm that you knew he was selling drugs to her."

Every time I thought about that night, my insides twisted into a knot. My sister wasn't high when I left that night. I'd unfortunately become familiar with how she looked and behaved when she was high. She'd looked a little tired, but okay.

"As to what happens next, we already have a warrant ready to go. He's not the only person being arrested," Officer Blankenship explained. My heart started beating unsteadily and dread coated my insides. "We expect to file a warrant with the court soon. He'll be arrested along with the others."

I swallowed. Janet was patiently sitting beside me, her presence soothing me. "So, uh, will this be public information?"

"Yes. If you'd like, I can notify you when he's in custody. I'm assuming you'll want to communicate with your parents at that point."

My tears felt cold on my cheeks as I nodded, before replying, "Yes." My voice was hoarse and my heart literally ached.

When I finished the call, Janet scooted her chair closer and wrapped her arm around my shoulder, giving me a squeeze before handing me a tissue. "I heard most of it. I know this is painful, but I think it's for the best. Your sister deserves justice."

I took a shaky breath, followed by a swallow of coffee, needing the jolt of caffeine and the rich flavor to knock my system out of its dazed shock. "It hurts, but it's a relief."

Josie and Janet kept checking on me as the afternoon went along. Even though all of this was stressful, I felt a little lighter inside without the weight of feeling alone in what I suspected about how my sister died.

Chapter Twenty-Eight

CASEY

Over the next few days, I didn't know how to adjust to the news that Nathaniel was going to be arrested and charged. When I got the call from Officer Blankenship that he was in custody and the charges were public information, I burst into tears.

The truth finally might come out and I wouldn't have to carry the weight of my suspicions alone. My relief was short-lived because, of course, his parents bailed him out of jail.

My parents called and left me emotionally devastated.

"I simply cannot believe it," my mother said, her voice ringing with conviction.

"Mom, you know how Callie died. Just because you think you know someone doesn't mean you actually do," I said.

My father cut in, "I talked to Nathaniel as soon as he was out. They got the wrong guy. The police are connecting dots that don't even exist. He and your sister were never involved. You're the one he's been in love with for years."

It was amazing I didn't vomit on my phone. "Dad! He's not in love with me. He never has been. I have no idea why you would think that. I know he and Callie were seeing each other, and he was dealing her drugs. She told me! There are four deaths connected to drugs he sold. Don't be so naïve."

"Honey, you cannot believe that," my mother insisted. Her voice was a little shaky though, and I sensed cracks starting to form in her faith in Nathaniel.

"I do. I've suspected he had something to do with Callie's death ever since it happened. While I did always want to travel, finally coming to Alaska has been a relief. I'm far enough away from what happened to feel like I can breathe. Nathaniel knows I suspect something because he's been texting and calling me. I don't answer. While Callie is responsible for her own actions, he is responsible for selling her drugs that were too strong."

Tears were rolling down my cheeks, and I was shaking all over.

"He's innocent until proven guilty," my dad said.

I'd known my dad would struggle with this. He'd been horrified by what happened to my sister. He couldn't even believe my sister had gotten addicted to anything. He didn't understand addiction and how it affected people. He thought she'd been too strong for that to happen.

"Believe whatever you want. I'm confident Nathaniel is going to be proven guilty. I won't be surprised if he cuts a plea deal. If you want to honor Callie's memory, maybe you should think twice about who you believe." With shaking hands, I ended the call.

I missed Leo. I would've given anything for his strong embrace right now. I was relieved for work and the escape it offered. We were getting busier by the day. Janet had warned me I might think winter was busy, but once the tourists started pouring into town, the pace would increase exponentially.

Luna couldn't even keep up with the donut demand. At the end of another crazy day, I locked the front door and turned on some music while I cleaned. It was quiet, and Leo strolled into my thoughts. It was late evening after closing time when he'd stopped by for that late coffee and spilled it all over me.

I'd give just about anything to see him right now. When I

fetched my purse from the back and checked my phone, I felt as if I were falling. There was a slew of text messages from Nathaniel. While he didn't directly incriminate himself, he was furious I'd spoken to the police. His final message was like a blast of icy cold water.

You'd better not testify against me. You'd better fucking tell them you must've misunderstood. You might be far away, but I can make things really uncomfortable for your parents. It's not what you think.

My hands were shaking when the back door to the café opened. Josie poked her head in, her brown curls bouncing around her shoulders as she smiled over at me. "Hey, what—" she began.

She stepped inside, quickly pulling the door shut when she saw my expression. "What's going on?"

I burst into tears. I'd been doing that frequently ever since the phone call from Officer Blankenship. Josie got me some tissues and sat me down in the break room. She already knew the outlines of the situation, so all I did was show her the series of texts.

After she read through them, she looked up, fury flashing in her eyes. "Fuck him! He can't do anything to you."

I held her gaze and took a slow breath. "I know, but he can make my parents miserable just by messing with their guilt and the fact that they love him like a son."

"Maybe so, but eventually, they'll believe it. The courts don't approve warrants unless they have a good case. Who gives a shit if he's out on bail? He's threatening you because he's worried. It's not like they built their case on your information." She held my gaze and reached for my hands. "This is going to be okay. Callie is going to have justice."

I breathed in slowly, almost feeling as if I was inhaling her strength as she squeezed my hands. "Okay."

"Your hands are freezing," she pointed out.

"I get cold when I'm anxious."

"This calls for a steaming hot cup of coffee or tea," she announced. "What's your preference?"

I blinked away my tears and looked at my friend. "Chai tea."

"Coming right up!" She bounced up and hurried to the front.

Chapter Twenty-Nine

LEO

I dropped my heavy bag of gear on the ground beside a fallen log and sat down with a sigh. Resting my elbows on my knees, I glanced over at Hudson and Graham. "We made it."

Graham chuckled, offering a tired smile. "We always do."

Hudson kicked his feet out in front of him and reached for a water bottle on the ground, taking a long swallow as he nodded.

"Any idea when we might get picked up?" I asked.

Graham lifted his gaze to the sky. "Sometime," he quipped.

A weary laugh rustled in my throat. I whisked my gaze around the sky. There was still some smoke in the distance, but the remains of the fire were smoldering on the now-wet ground. We'd been out here two full weeks. Dry weather and wind had continued to whip the fire up, while we stayed busy cutting lines of protection and trying to box the fire in. A conveniently located river and some welcome rain for the last two days had finally helped us finish the job.

The fire was considered fully contained now and would be monitored from the air. Although the vast wilderness of Alaska offered plenty of places for fires to burn wild, there were small planes crisscrossing the skies here daily. Between those and drones, they monitored the backcountry and reported on fires.

"You ready to get home?" I asked Graham. "How do you manage being gone with a toddler at home?"

Graham finished chewing a granola bar before tilting his head to the side as he considered me. "Well, I have Madison at home. And, Allie," he said, referring to his college-aged daughter. "It was just me when Allie was younger, so I was on the town crew. You've got your parents, so I'm sure that helps a lot."

"I don't know. Even though I have my parents to help when I'm gone, this whole thing is unexpected. I want her to feel like I'm there for her."

Graham nodded. "It's quality, not quantity. How's Dora doing?"

"I've never had a kid, so I'm not sure. She seems to be adjusting well. Even with my job, I think her life is more stable than it was with her mom."

Parker approached, plunking down on the ground beside Hudson and asking, "Any water? I'm all out."

Hudson reached into his backpack and handed over a bottle of water. Griffin joined us a moment later, dragging his sleeve across his forehead with a sigh after he dropped his heavy gear bag on the ground. "I am ready to go home," he announced as he sat down on the ground across from me.

"Safe to say, all of us are," I offered dryly.

"Ask Griffin about life with a young kid," Graham chimed in.

Griffin glanced over. "Huh?"

"Leo was asking how I used to handle being a firefighter when Allie was young. She's all grown up and I have Madison to help now. What do you think about traveling as a hotshot with a baby at home?" Graham asked.

Griffin tipped his head to the side before a smile stretched across his face. "Best thing ever. Coming home is awesome. I love seeing Tish, but having a toddler makes it even better. Teddy is fucking ecstatic to see me. He made me a drawing last time."

"That is sweet," Parker said with a grin.

"Dora's been staying with my parents. This is the job I had when I found out she existed, and I worry if it's okay. I don't know what to think sometimes," I explained.

"Kids are pretty resilient," Graham offered. "I don't mean to make it seem like it's no big deal, but when Allie was little her mom was barely around. I think Allie's turned out pretty good. My best suggestion is to communicate consistently about whatever the situation is. Work, life, and so on."

"Dora's mom passed away, so—" I let out a sigh, running a hand through my hair.

Parker nudged me with his shoulder from the side. "It'll be okay. Maybe it doesn't seem like it now, but she's got you and your parents."

"It doesn't seem like much." The doubts pinging around in my thoughts felt like a pinball machine gone wild.

"Okay, listen. I'm serious," Parker chimed in. "My mom flaked when I was little. My dad wasn't all that stable, but he loved me. By stable, I mean he didn't make great choices and bounced in and out of jail a little bit."

Hudson caught my eyes. "Mine too. We ended up in juvenile detention together thanks to our fathers kind of falling down on teaching us how to make good decisions in high school. My mom wasn't around either. We turned out okay."

"And we both have decent relationships with our dads now," Parker added. "Maybe they weren't too stable, but they loved us and that made all the difference. That's the key. For what it's worth, I'm not pretending like it's simple. I know plenty of people who had good parents and turned out being train wrecks once they were adults, but being there for her can make all the difference in the world."

Graham smiled over at me. "This all started because Leo's wondering if he should switch to the town crew."

Hudson shrugged. "That's a six of one, half a dozen of the other kind of thing. You're still gonna get called out randomly with the town crew. As a hotshot, you'll be gone for chunks of time, but it's not all the time. In the winter, you're mostly home."

"Or, follow Beck's advice and fall in love," Griffin offered with a chuckle.

"And get married, or at least, shack up," Graham added dryly.

I snorted. Beck was known for his strong opinions on happily ever after. Of course, I hadn't talked to the guys about the fact that I was pretty much in love with Casey.

As if he could see right into my brain, Hudson piped up, "You and Casey are seeing each other. Are you serious enough that she's met Dora?"

A chuckle rustled in my throat. "She's met Dora and my parents."

"Holy smokes." Graham let out a whistle. "You're in love. Is Casey ready to sign on for being a stepparent?"

Chapter Thirty

LEO

Along with the rain came some wind, which delayed our trip home. A full day later, I walked out of the station. I fished my phone out of my pocket, re-reading Casey's text.

Casey: It's a work day for me at Firehouse Café, but I'd love to see you!

As soon as we'd gotten into cell range when we were flying back, I'd called Dora and my parents and left Casey a message.

Me: Heading home to see Dora, then I'll stop by the café. Might have her with me.

When I got home, Dora flung herself at my legs, hugging them. My heart squeezed tightly as I knelt down to hug her.

"You're home!" my daughter exclaimed when she finally let go.

"I sure am." I squeezed her shoulders.

"The cats are fine," she announced.

I chuckled as I glanced down at the cats. One of them was sniffing my boots and the other was twining around Dora's ankles.

"Looks like you took good care of them."

She nodded, her braids swinging with the motion. She proceeded to talk in a run-on sentence for the next ten minutes straight. I got a minute-by-minute summary of the last few days. My mom was in the kitchen, tidying up from a snack she'd just made for Dora. She smiled at me at one point, her eyes warm.

Eventually, Dora ran out of words and stopped to take a deep breath before asking, "Are you going to see Casey? Grammy took me to see her yesterday and I told her I missed you and she said she missed you too."

I chuckled. "Of course. Would you like to go with me?"

Dora squealed, bouncing up and down and clapping her hands.

"I take it that means yes," I teased.

My mom gave Dora a hug and a wave, and off we went.

———

A small downside to having a child was I wanted Casey all to myself tonight, but that wasn't an option. As I held her close and breathed her in, I had to bite my tongue to keep from telling her I loved her.

Dora wasn't even shy. She smiled up at Casey. "Are you going to have a slumber party with Daddy tonight?"

Janet was behind the counter and snorted, while Josie waggled her brows when Casey's cheeks turned bright pink.

"I'm not sure about that," Casey finally hedged.

"I'm sure Daddy's gonna say maybe he shouldn't, but I think you should just come stay. We can watch my favorite show together," Dora said, swinging her arms back and forth.

I looked down at Dora. "We'll figure that out later, okay?"

Janet walked around the counter, reaching for Dora's hand. "I want to take her on a tour of the kitchen. We have fresh donuts."

"Can I have a donut?" Dora promptly asked.

"You sure can," Janet replied with a chuckle.

Josie handed me a coffee and shooed us over to sit at a table.

When I sat down across from Casey, she blurted out, "Should I stay? That was a lot, and I missed you."

"I missed you too." I reached for her hands, squeezing them before leaning across and giving her a kiss. I wanted a lot more than a kiss, but we were in public. I reluctantly leaned back and took a swallow of my coffee after I released her hands. I couldn't say why, but I sensed she was worried about something. "Everything okay?"

She lifted a shoulder in a small shrug. "Pretty much. You're going to hear about it. Josie, Luna, and Janet know the whole story. An officer from North Carolina called. There's a whole investigation involving Nathaniel, and he was arrested."

"Oh? Is he in jail?"

"He's out on bail. It's just stressful."

I studied her, taking in the tight lines around her mouth, the worry flickering in her eyes. I wanted to hold her close, to protect her, to make it all better.

"Is there anything I can do?"

Chapter Thirty-One

CASEY

Leo's helpful question kept boomeranging back in my thoughts. I honestly didn't know how he could help. I tried to ignore the niggling worry that somehow Nathaniel could harm me, my parents, Leo, or worst of all, Dora. I didn't mean in the physical sense, but I didn't know what he was capable of. When people were desperate, sometimes they made desperate choices.

And yet, with all of those worries simmering in the background, it was good, *so, so* good to have Leo home. We stayed with the schedule we'd had before he was out of town with me spending the night on Fridays when Dora had her TV night and stayed over at her grandparents' house.

The week he returned, that meant a wait since he got back on a Tuesday. He came to see me every day at the café while I waited patiently for Friday to arrive. When Stella stopped by to see me, I was beyond relieved that she invited me to another card night. It gave me something to do. I was still occasionally doing delivery for the local pizza place, but that was sporadic.

Stella's blonde curls were pulled up in a messy ponytail as she smiled at me. "Tonight?" I prompted as I slid the chai tea she'd ordered across the counter to her.

"Do you have plans with Leo?" She took a swallow of her tea, letting out a happy sigh when she lowered the cup. "Delicious."

"I wish I had plans with Leo." I bit back an impatient sigh. "I have to wait until Friday."

"You should move in with him," she declared.

"I can't just move in with him! He has a daughter. Dora's met me, but we have to take it one step at a time."

"I get it. Maybe you should have a quickie somewhere in the car, or something," she teased.

"Stella!"

She giggled. "You gotta do what you gotta do."

The door to the café swung open, and Leo came walking in with Beck, Hudson, and Griffin. My pulse took off as if it was racing to win a medal, while my hormones let out a rousing cheer at the sight of Leo.

Hudson stopped beside Stella, leaning down to kiss her on her cheek. Meanwhile, Beck glanced between us. "What's so funny?"

My cheeks got hot when Stella's eyes slid to mine. She gave a saucy shrug. "Nothing."

When Leo's gaze collided with mine, my face burned even hotter. Stella looked right at him as she said, "Your truck is great."

Hudson gave her a puzzled look. "What's so great about Leo's truck?"

I burst out laughing. Beck glanced around the group and rolled his eyes. "I know what's so great about Leo's truck."

Leo glanced at him. "You do?"

"Well?" Stella prompted with a brow waggle and a teasing grin as we watched Maisie win another game.

"Well, what?" I hedged.

"Leo and his truck," she replied.

"What about Leo's truck?" Tish asked while Susannah looked between us curiously.

I tried to will my blush away, but it was pointless. My cheeks were on fire.

"Leo just got back with the rest of his crew, and Casey is waiting for Friday because, I guess, that's the only night she goes over there. Which I support from a practical stance, by the way," Stella explained.

"Ohhhh," Tish said slowly.

Susannah chuckled. "Important to be appropriate when there's a child involved. Why is Friday special?" she asked while she waited for Lucy to finish shuffling the cards.

"Because Dora watches a TV show with her grandmother and stays over there for the night."

"I suggested a quickie in Leo's truck," Stella offered with a sly grin.

My friends collectively giggled at that.

"I'm not opposed to it," I finally said. "But I'm not going to report back."

"Nothing wrong with a little privacy," Tish said dryly.

By the time Friday rolled around, I was beyond impatient. Things had been blessedly quiet as far as hearing anything else from my parents, or Nathaniel. Officer Blankenship told me they were in a holding pattern with the case moving forward as the prosecution team negotiated with the various attorneys involved.

Leo had texted me he wanted to take me out to dinner. Initially, I thought that meant we'd be going out to dinner with Dora and his parents. When he picked me up, I asked, "Are they meeting us there?"

He slid his gaze to mine as he shook his head.

"Dora?"

His smile was slow and sent my belly into a swoop. "Just you and me, sweetheart," he murmured as he leaned across the console to kiss me.

By the time he lifted his head, I was breathless with heat

pooling low in my belly. I felt liquid all over. I was relieved I was sitting down because no doubt my knees would've given out otherwise. As it was, I needed time to recover.

"Oh. Is that okay?" I belatedly asked a moment later.

Leo pulled out of the parking area. "Is what okay?"

"Don't you usually have dinner with Dora and your parents on Friday before she stays over there?"

"Not always. When Dora first came to me in Juneau, I didn't even have a bedroom for her. She stayed with my parents for a little while. When I decided to move here because the job opened up, it was ideal for them to finally move back completely and keep up with one overnight a week. That way, Dora's comfortable there." His eyes slid to mine as he slowed to turn down a side road off of Main Street. "Now that I'm seeing you, it makes for a convenient night for us to do something. We can have dinner with them sometimes, but it's not a requirement."

"What did you do on Fridays before we met?"

"Sometimes I had dinner with them, sometimes I went out with the guys. Sometimes I just hung out at my place and relaxed."

He reached over, squeezing my knee, the brief touch sending heat and sparks scattering through me.

I tried to breathe. "Where are we going?"

"I thought we'd go to Fireweed Winery. Is that okay?"

"Of course! I love good food, and I've heard the winery is amazing."

A few minutes later, Leo slowed to a stop while we waited for a moose and two calves to cross the road. I smiled as I watched them. While the mama moose looked like she was ambling, her calves were hurrying to keep pace.

"I never could've imagined how often I would see moose here. It's wild," I said with a little laugh.

Leo chuckled as he waited until they fully crossed the road before beginning to drive forward again. "They're pretty much everywhere."

"I haven't seen a grizzly bear yet though, and I've decided I'm fine with that."

"Yeah?" he prompted as he turned into the parking area for Fireweed Winery.

"I saw one of the taxidermy ones at the airport. They're huge! Once, when I went out to the transfer station, I saw the tracks for one. Their claws are so long that they wouldn't even have to be trying to hurt you to really hurt you."

"They don't want to encounter humans either. They're just living their life being bears," Leo said wryly. "If you ever wanted to see them, we could fly over to Katmai Park. They have the viewing platforms there, and it's pretty safe."

A short while later, we were in the restaurant and I glanced around. "Until I moved here, I didn't realize Fireweed Industries was from Alaska. They're kind of a big deal."

Leo flashed a smile. "When I was growing up, they ran a mine in Willow Brook. That shut down, right about when my parents moved to Juneau. Their winery and brewery started the whole thing. They're kind of the craft beer equivalent of one of the big beer places. Once that took off, they kept expanding into other things. Their flagship distribution place and restaurant are in Fireweed Harbor. It's nice they opened this here. I'm hoping they're going to start doing local's night like they do in Fireweed Harbor."

"What do they do for that?"

"Discounts in the restaurant for locals. The best part is you get to taste test their wines and beers, including ones that aren't officially in production yet." Leo waggled his brows. "It's fun."

I took a swallow from the raspberry honey mead I'd ordered. "Well, this is amazing."

Aside from the food, which was delicious, it was nice to spend time with Leo. I knew I was in love with him, but I also liked him. He was easy to be with. I didn't have to think about conversation.

After dinner, we went back to his place. Once we walked into his house, he shut the door behind us and turned to face me. When his gaze locked with mine, butterflies tickled my belly and a wave of sparks scattered through me. My knees were wobbly, and I pressed my palms against the door behind me, grateful for the support.

"I missed you," he said, his voice gravelly.

Chapter Thirty-Two

CASEY

Sweet hell. The mere sound of Leo's voice got to me. I'd never paid much attention to the sound of anyone's voice. I'd certainly never experienced a man's voice making me practically swoon at his feet.

"I missed you too," I whispered.

Leo lifted a hand, brushing a wayward lock of hair off my cheek. The subtle brush of his touch against my skin was a blaze of heat. His fingertips glanced over the sensitive skin on my earlobe. I swallowed, trying to suck in enough air. I licked my lips. He took a step closer and I felt his heat and strength envelop me.

His palm landed on the door beside my shoulder. It felt as if everything was moving in slow motion as he dipped his head. Just as his lips brushed against mine, he whispered, "I'm so glad to be home."

We tumbled into the fire together. A little while later, I fell asleep, warm and sated, my heart feeling as if it was home. The following morning, after Leo's mother brought Dora home, Dora announced, "I want donuts."

"I know where you can get the very best donuts," I said as she looked up at me.

"Firehouse Café," she said, nodding vigorously.

I grinned. "My friend Luna makes them."

Dora bounced up and down. "When can we go?"

Leo chuckled. "How about now?"

After she checked on the cats who were happily napping in a patch of sunshine, Dora skipped over to the door. Once we were at the café, we went into the back so Luna could show her what the donuts looked like when they were fresh out of the oven.

"What kind do you want?" Janet asked a few minutes later.

Dora was completely undecided. "I want them all, the sugar, the cinnamon, and the chocolate and—" She ran out of breath.

Leo curled his palm over her shoulder, squeezing gently. "We can come back to try different flavors every week."

Dora let out a tiny sigh and nodded somberly. "Today, I am in the mood for the sprinkles."

After we were seated at a table, Leo caught my eye while Dora happily ate her donut. My heart twisted in my chest with a piercing sense of joy.

Later that day, my phone rang, and my anxiety spun wild inside. When my parents called, it felt as if the quicksand of grief was pulling me in deeper.

"Nathaniel has an excellent attorney. He's going to beat these charges," my dad said confidently.

"Dad, why would you want that?" I asked sharply.

"Because he didn't do this. We talked to him. There's no way he would be involved in something like this," my mother answered.

With the barely healed scabs on my heart over Callie's death, I sat on that call with tears rolling down my cheeks, wanting to scream and cry and shake them.

I finally broke. "I cannot believe you would protect someone who might be involved in Callie's death."

. . .

"Casey, there's no way!" my mother scolded.

I drew in a shaky breath. "People do things we don't expect. You didn't believe that Callie was doing drugs until you got the toxicology report after she died. Nathaniel has never been a saint."

Chapter Thirty-Three

LEO

"Where is Casey?" Dora asked. Her eyes were hopeful as she looked ahead at the counter in Firehouse Café.

"I don't think she's working today," I answered when we stopped in front of the counter.

As I glanced down at Dora when she placed her hands on the counter, I marveled that it seemed like she was growing almost every day. Her chin was now above the counter. Her eyes scanned the chalkboard above. My heart almost ached when she mouthed the words to herself. She *loved* to read.

She didn't even like me to read her bedtime stories. She preferred to read them herself. The library was one of her favorite places to go.

The door to the kitchen swung open, and Janet came walking out. Her eyes caught mine first before she looked down at Dora, her smile stretching wide. "Hello, Miss Dora." Janet leaned down, resting her elbows on the counter so she was close to eye level with Dora. "How are you today?"

Dora giggled. "Good. How are you?" She swayed on her feet, swinging her arms.

Janet tapped her fingertips on the counter as she straightened up, appearing to seriously consider Dora's question. "I'm doing well today." She glanced toward me. "And, how are you, Leo?"

"I'm also doing well." I grinned at her, placing my hands on Dora's shoulders.

"What can I get you two?"

I ordered a coffee, and Dora ordered hot chocolate. "Can I get a donut?" Her eyes bounced up to mine.

"You sure can."

She carefully selected one, while I got a whole box for the guys at the station.

"Where is Casey?" Dora asked Janet as I was paying a few minutes later.

"She's not working until this afternoon," Janet replied.

"Oh." Dora's brow squinched with disappointment.

I couldn't quite pin it down, but Casey seemed to be pulling back a little and I wasn't sure how to interpret that.

I wanted a chance to talk to her about it, but I had Dora every night before Friday. We were still in the only Friday nights together phase. I honestly wanted to change that, but I wasn't sure when the timing was right. We actually had an appointment with our therapist today. I planned to bring it up to get her feedback.

Chapter Thirty-Four

LEO

Our therapist looked between us. Every so often, I almost burst out laughing at these appointments. It all started as a joke. Casey didn't even talk much about why she dragged me in there to be her fake fiancé. Now that we were actually a couple and we'd fessed up to our therapist about how the whole thing started, I honestly thought, if her parents showed up in town, I could roll with it and pretend like we were engaged.

There'd been a time in my life when the idea of being engaged to anyone would've given me hives. Ever since Dora had come into my life, I truly hadn't had time to think about relationships. And yet, I wanted my engagement to Casey to be more than fake.

"So, you're trying to figure out the timing for when Casey can actually spend the night at your house when Dora is there?" Delaney prompted.

I took a slow breath. "I am. By the way, I feel like there should be an instruction manual for parenting. There are so many unknown factors. Whenever I ask people for feedback, everybody gives me a different answer." I lifted my gaze to Delaney. "You're the expert. Tell me what to do, how to handle this part."

She laughed softly, and I started to laugh with her. When I glanced toward Casey and saw her hands twisting in her lap, I knew something was amiss.

"What's going on with you, Casey? You seem nervous and I don't sense it's about when to stay over at Leo's house." Delaney's gaze instantly sobered.

Casey's breath drew in quickly. She turned to look at me, tears shimmering in her eyes. "I think it's okay if we don't know yet and we wait. I didn't know how to talk to you about this, but Nathaniel's still out on bail. My parents think he's going to win the case. He sent me a message that felt threatening. I just... I don't want anything to happen to Dora."

Anger and fear slammed into my chest. It felt like someone had literally punched me, directly over my heart. "Casey, he can't hurt Dora or me. He's in North Carolina."

She twisted her hands again. "My parents don't believe he's had any involvement. I don't know how to get them to understand, or believe me."

"What does this mean for us?" I pressed.

"You and Dora mean a lot to me, and I don't want to mess this up. I need to make sure he can't cause any problems."

"What is he doing, Casey?" Delaney chimed in.

Casey burst into tears. Over the next few minutes, between sniffles, blowing her nose, and wiping her eyes with tissues, Casey explained that Nathaniel had texted her and was threatening to somehow cause problems for her father. "Nathaniel told me not to talk to the police, but I already did, and I don't know what to do."

Delaney was quiet for a few moments before she gently offered, "It makes sense that you'd be afraid. I can't tell you what to do, but I think you should talk to the police officer about what's happening."

Casey looked toward me, and I felt all twisted up inside. I wanted to help her, but it felt like she was trying to keep me at bay.

"What do you think I should do?" she asked.

"Let me help you."

Chapter Thirty-Five

CASEY

Let me help you.

Every time Leo's words circled through my thoughts, I had to blink away tears.

I was relieved I had to go to work at the café early because it kept me from dwelling too much. The days were starting to get longer and it was wild to me how long the sun stayed up. It was only May, and sunrise was before six a.m. with sunset after ten p.m. at night.

The café was still and quiet at five in the morning. I loved arriving here so early. My short walk from my apartment next door was beautiful with the air crisp and fresh and the sky awash in tangerine and gold. The snow was still melting on the top of the mountains. With that, there was lots of chatter about mud season, something I'd never experienced. Since I lived and worked downtown, I didn't notice it all that much, although I did see lots of muddy yards when I was driving. There were also plenty of people tromping mud into the café.

Josie insisted she had to take me out for a hike so I could experience mud season in all its glory. There was also lots of talk about betting on when the ice would crack on the rivers. I loved

Alaska and I loved Willow Brook. I was startled to discover it already felt like home. I truly felt like I belonged here.

Ever since I'd started my travels across the United States, I'd wondered if I would fall in love with any area. The salty breezes in coastal North Carolina lived in my heart and always would. Alaska was the only other place that felt like home. Oddly, it felt even more like home to me than North Carolina had. Alaska had been the last place on my bucket list.

I'd traveled to New England during the stunning beauty of autumn. I'd hiked in the White Mountains and the Green Mountains. I'd driven through the Adirondacks and the Catskills. Niagara Falls had taken my breath away with a sense of wonder and awe. I'd driven through the Midwest, enjoying the wind in the grasses and the way the sunset wowed me. I'd watched a storm coming from miles and miles away on the flat landscape. Upper Michigan had been a sweet surprise. No one had told me how pretty it was. The Great Lakes lived up to their name. They were so big it almost felt like standing on the shore of the ocean.

I'd headed south again and passed through the Badlands of South Dakota, all the way to the Grand Canyon, yet another breathtaking place. The redwoods of California made me feel like a tiny speck in the universe, and the Pacific Northwest was a lush area.

That was the last stop before I made my way to Alaska. The drive to Alaska was filled with vast beauty. It was also longer than I'd expected and offered plenty of wildlife to see. I'd seen mountain goats and grizzly bears from a distance, along with moose, caribou, wolves, coyotes, and more birds than I could count.

When I stopped in Anchorage and asked about nearby towns, Willow Brook came up repeatedly. It was rumored to have good restaurants, an art gallery, and lots of summer jobs. I'd been so tired the night I made it here. My choice to stop at Firehouse Café opened a doorway into a new life and a place where I felt I belonged.

I could tell Luna had already been here this morning with trays of donuts ready to go into the oven soon. I puttered around in the kitchen, heating up a leftover ham and cheese twist before heading to the front to make an espresso with a dash of dark chocolate in it while I got ready to open.

All the while, my heart ached a little. I worried that somehow Nathaniel was going to steal the peace I'd started to find. I didn't honestly know how Leo could help me with any of this mess.

I heard the door to the kitchen open, followed by Luna's voice calling out, "Hey, it's me!"

"Hey! Want a coffee?"

Luna appeared over the waist-high swinging door from the back, her cheeks pink from the cool air as she smiled at me. "The answer is always yes," she teased. "I'm going to put the donuts in the oven."

I got her coffee ready, and a few minutes later, we sat together in the back. I liked Luna and felt lucky to be her friend. She was quirky and sweet and carried a sense of protective warmth. Whenever I was with her, I felt like somehow everything would be okay.

With her hands curled around her mug, she looked over at me. "What's wrong?"

"What do you mean?" I hedged.

Her big eyes blinked. "You don't have to tell me, but I'm worried. You've been looking sad and anxious for days now."

My throat felt thick and my chest tight. I blinked to keep the tears from rolling down my cheeks. "I'm sorry. I'm so used to keeping everything to myself and—" My words ended abruptly. I took a quick breath, trying to loosen the anxiety that was starting to spin like a storm inside.

She set her mug down, leaning across the table and reaching

for my hands with hers. "You don't have to talk about it, but if you want to, I'm here."

I swallowed and took a shaky breath before the whole story poured out. Luna already knew the general details of what happened to my sister, but I'd been holding in all the stress around Nathaniel.

"You need to tell Officer Blankenship about those texts from him," she insisted. "Don't wait on this. Because if you wait, you're just giving Nathaniel time to muck things up."

"I know, I know. Leo wants to help, but there's nothing he can do. I don't want to break up with him, but he has Dora to think about. He doesn't need to be worrying about this."

Luna was sipping her coffee again and tipped her head to the side. "Casey, let Leo be there for you. What will that hurt?"

I shrugged. "I just feel like I need this resolved before more can happen with us. I worry about Dora." I didn't know how to explain it, but there was a lingering fear I couldn't banish. Maybe it was because Nathaniel had already taken one person I loved.

Luna's nose wrinkled, her ponytail bouncing as she nodded. "After everything she's been through, I understand."

"Talk to Leo about it. Better yet, talk about it with your therapist." She paused, laughing a little at this. "You two have a couples therapist because you dragged him into that appointment."

Her comment lightened the moment, and I giggled. "I have *no* idea what I was thinking that day."

Luna shrugged. "It's not the craziest thing to do." Her gaze sobered. "In all honesty, knowing what you've been carrying about your sister and the pressure from your parents, I don't blame you. I'd make up a fiancé too just to get them to shut the fuck up. As painful as it is that your parents are struggling to believe how Nathaniel was involved, denial is a coping skill, even if it's not healthy. Eventually, the whole truth will come out."

Her observation echoed in my thoughts when I played a message from my parents later.

"We're coming to visit! We decided it was time. See you soon!"

Dora peered up at me with her hands on her hips. "They need a bed."

It was amazing how quickly I had come to know her little traits. Hands on hips meant she was prepared to put up a fight about something. In this case, it was totally unnecessary. If she wanted a bed for the cats, it was a done deal.

"We'll pick out a bed for them," I said simply.

When her brows hitched up in surprise, my heart twisted in my chest. I would never know all that she experienced with her mom, but I had enough sense to recognize money had been tight. I wasn't rich by any means, but I could cover the bills and buy cat beds. Those were the things that mattered.

Dora's hands fell from her hips. She blinked up at me before her face cracked into a wide smile. "Yay!" She clapped her hands together. "When can we go?"

I glanced at my watch. "Now?"

"Yes, please."

Off we went. Although Willow Brook had grown some recently, it was still a small town and always would be. Our options for cat bed shopping were the grocery store's pet section and the small pet selection at the local hardware store. I decided we should try our luck at the grocery store first because I could get groceries at the same time.

"This one!" Dora announced a little while later at the grocery store. "Can we get two?"

At my nod, she selected two cat beds. They were pink with sparkly stars on them. I didn't think the cats cared about the color, but Dora sure did. After that, we did a loop through the store, and I picked up some groceries for the upcoming week. After we brought everything back to the house and she supervised the cats as they inspected their new beds, Dora asked to go to Firehouse Café.

"To see Casey," she explained as she looked up at me. "Are you having a slumber party with her tonight?"

I glanced at Dora. "Excuse me?"

"That's what you do. I have a slumber party with Grammy and you have a slumber party with Casey."

I bit back a sigh. Moments like this made me want that instruction manual. What was I supposed to say? Technically, she was accurate. I recalled back when Dora first came to stay with me that her therapist in Juneau had recommended to be honest whenever I could, even if it was awkward. Delaney had reinforced that, clarifying that sometimes kids would guess things and it was important to provide the information in a neutral, honest way.

I held Dora's gaze. "Sometimes. How do you feel about that?"

"Well, I want you to marry Casey, so I feel good about that," she said matter-of-factly.

Oh, fuck.

Scrambling mentally, I cleared my throat. "Well, uh, I don't know if Casey and I are having a slumber party tonight. But we can go into Firehouse Café and maybe we'll see her."

Dora cocked her head to the side, scrunching her nose up as she considered this. "You don't know if she'll be there?"

"I don't. She's not always there. Sometimes, Janet, or Josie, or Luna is working."

"Oh, okay."

Dora said an elaborate goodbye to the cats and got her bucket purse.

A little while later, we were in the thick of an awkward situation. Casey's smile was beyond strained, and her parents were there with Nathaniel and his parents. Dora had blinked up at Casey and asked her if she was okay, but Janet blessedly kept her occupied by bringing chalk and markers over to our table for her.

When I got up to go to the restroom, I was trying to figure out how to get a moment alone with Casey. Janet caught me by the elbow. "What is it?" I asked.

"I think you need to do your thing," she whispered.

"My thing?"

"You're Casey's pretend fiancé. I think you need to make it really convincing right now."

Chapter Thirty-Seven

CASEY

I was trying so hard to keep it together I worried I might splinter apart. While I'd known my parents were coming for a visit, they'd left out that they were bringing along Nathaniel and his parents. They had vacationed together many times, so that wasn't unusual, but I hadn't expected them to bring him here. I didn't know how to contain the distress I felt.

I'd somehow fumbled my way through when they showed up last night. Blessedly, I had a one-bedroom apartment, so they didn't expect to stay with me. Now, they were here and Nathaniel was faking nice, but I could feel the undercurrent of anger from him.

My eyes kept darting over to Dora and Leo. I was in the middle of waiting on a customer when my mom appeared in the line again. When she got to the front, she smiled brightly. "So what do you think, honey? We would love for you to take us on a tour of town and then have dinner. And, are we going to be able to meet Leo?"

As if on cue, he appeared behind her in line just before rounding the counter to stand beside me. He curled his arm around my shoulders and planted a big kiss on my cheek. "You must be Casey's mother."

My mom's eyes locked on Leo. Her smile was bright, but I could see the questions swirling. "Leo! Casey's mysterious fiancé."

"That's me," he returned smoothly. I felt his palm slide down to rest on my hip, and he gave me a reassuring squeeze. Unsettled and distressed as I felt inside, his strong presence was soothing.

"I was just saying to Casey that we would love for her to have dinner with us tonight. Maybe you can join us too." My mother paused, her gaze sobering. "We could only get approval for a three-day trip for Nathaniel due to his conditions of release." Her eyes darted over to him, the fucking asshole. "He's dealing with some legal problems. It's all a big misunderstanding," my mother said, nodding, almost as if she were trying to reassure herself.

I wanted to cry.

"I'd love to join you all. When do you fly out?" Leo asked.

"The day after tomorrow. We just arrived late last night. It is a long flight from the East Coast to Alaska."

"Oh, it certainly is," Leo replied. "How about we meet at Fireweed Winery? I'll pick Casey up, and we can meet you all there."

"Of course. What time do you get off work, honey?" my mom asked.

Janet appeared beside me. I was in such a mental haze I didn't even know she had rounded the counter. "She's on duty until five-thirty."

That was a lie, but I decided to roll with it. I honestly just wanted to work the whole time my parents were here. I definitely didn't want to spend much time with them under the circumstances.

"Let's meet at six," Leo suggested.

"Excellent."

Nathaniel came walking up with his parents and my dad, and I wanted to cry all over again. Leo didn't move. When I glanced to where Dora was, I noticed Luna was with her. She was showing her tarot cards, and Dora appeared completely engrossed.

My mom was busy introducing Leo to Nathaniel, my dad, and Nathaniel's parents. I could feel the tension hovering in the air. With my emotions rioting inside, I was fighting tears combined with fury. I didn't understand what Nathaniel thought he could get out of this.

I was beyond relieved Leo was here. The comfort of his strength and protectiveness was the only thing that got me through these moments. After they all left, Leo leaned close, his arm still around my waist. "It's gonna be okay. I need you to trust me."

I looked up at him. His steady gaze held mine, and my anxiety slowed. "Okay," I whispered. "You don't have to do this, Leo."

"Maybe now isn't the time to say this, but I love you, Casey. This isn't about what I have to do, it's about what I want to do."

My heart thrashed in my chest as I stared at him, while joy rose through the clamor of other emotions crowding inside. "I love you too," I whispered.

The moment was snapped when Dora's voice broke through. "Daddy!" She was standing across the counter as we both turned to look at her.

Leo smiled. "Yes?"

"Luna says I can taste-test a donut, but I have to ask you if I can go in the back," Dora explained.

"Of course you can," he replied.

Luna's smile was reassuring when her eyes met mine. She held Dora's hand, leading her around the counter and into the kitchen in the back.

Customers started to pile up behind the counter, so Janet hopped into motion while Leo turned me to face him again. "I'll pick you up."

"Okay. Just pick me up here."

I didn't want there to be any opportunity for Nathaniel to catch me alone, so I planned to stay here all day.

"You got it."

He dipped his head to give me a quick kiss. After he left, I held onto those moments with him like a raft in choppy waters.

Chapter Thirty-Eight

LEO

That evening, I sat beside Casey at dinner at Fireweed Winery. I had to give it to Nathaniel. The man could bullshit with the best of them.

He was smooth with sweet talking his parents and Casey's. He even had the nerve to lament what a mess it was that he had accidentally been swept up in this criminal case just because he happened to know some of the people involved.

If I'd been more of an asshole, I would've brought up Casey's sister, but I couldn't bring myself to do so, not with her and her parents here.

His parents started droning on about how unfair it was and how they just could *not* even believe they had to get permission for him to travel. At that point, Casey's parents jumped on that bandwagon. I was plain furious.

I held Casey's hand under the table, and I could feel the tension vibrating through her. She was sad and angry, but she was holding it together. I wanted to slay every dragon she faced. At the moment, that happened to be a table full of people who claimed to love her.

I couldn't figure out how Nathaniel thought he could implicate Casey's father in this and how he would stop Casey from testifying. I felt like I was missing something. When Nathaniel and his dad walked up to the bar together, I decided to be nosy.

After I squeezed Casey's hand, I cast a bland smile around the table. "I'll be right back. I'm gonna say hello to my friend who's bartending tonight."

I gave Casey a kiss on her cheek, leaning close enough to whisper, "Just checking on something. I promise it'll be okay."

I looped around to the back hallway and slipped into the storage area behind the bar, silently shouting a hallelujah when I encountered Delilah Blake. I hadn't been lying that my friend was working here tonight.

"Hey there," I said when her brows hitched up when she saw me.

Delilah's husband was a good friend. We'd grown up together, and I saw him often these days as he was an aviation mechanic and handled all the maintenance on the planes and helicopters that transported us out to fires.

"Hey, Leo," Delilah returned, a smile teasing at the corners of her mouth.

"I'm sure you're wondering why the hell I'm back here, so let me cut to the chase. There are two men at the bar waiting to be served." I quickly gave her Nathaniel's description. "I need you to eavesdrop for me and report back."

"You gonna fill me in on why?"

"Later. For now, I need you to not miss this opportunity. I'm not going to be here too long, so just text me."

Delilah threw a chuckle over her shoulder before slipping through the door that led to the back side of the bar. After that, I returned to the table, catching the tail end of Casey's mom enthusing about how much they liked Wildlands Lodge. "Are you seriously going to stay in Alaska for good?" she asked.

"I love Alaska, Mom," Casey replied.

I slipped into the chair beside her, interjecting, "And, we're engaged to be married." I took that comment as yet another opportunity to lay a kiss on Casey, this time going for her lips.

Her eyes were wide and dark and her cheeks a little pink when I lifted my head. Considering the level of tension tonight, I was relieved I could be a distraction. Nathaniel and his dad were talking at the bar with Delilah lingering right in front of them. Another bartender had joined her as well.

It was a solid ten minutes before Nathaniel and his father began walking back to the table. I was wondering if my request was worth it when I got a text from Delilah.

Bingo.

———

"You fucking asshole," I said, bluntly, staring straight at Nathaniel from across the table.

Nathaniel narrowed his eyes. "Do you normally just call your fiancé's old family friend an asshole?"

"I do when I find out why you're playing nice and bullshitting her parents about what you know you did. And, her father is paying for your attorney. I'll call you an asshole all I want," I said flatly.

Casey's mother glanced from her husband to Casey, to me, and to Nathaniel. Her brow furrowed. "We're old friends. We want to help him."

Casey's mouth dropped open and her fingers tightened around my hand where she held it under the table. "Dad! You can't afford that!"

Her dad looked a little embarrassed and also confused. "Honey, we just want Nathaniel to get out of this trouble. His parents definitely can't afford it."

Her mother looked toward me again. "Why are you asking about this and how do you even know?"

"Because they were at the bar talking about it. In fact—" I tipped my head toward Nathaniel's father. "He warned Nathaniel to keep Casey quiet, so you all don't find out everything. They know he's guilty."

Casey's eyes swung wildly around the table before finally landing on Nathaniel. "You are *such* an asshole. Mom, he was her dealer. He knows I know that. That's why he's been trying to bullshit this whole situation."

Nathaniel's expression was flat, but I could see the darkness in his eyes and his skin flushed to a ruddy shade. "That's bullshit, Casey."

"Is it though?" For the first time, she let her anger override the fear he'd instilled in her. "It's not. This whole game you've been playing that you always wanted a chance with me and all that stupid stuff, it was just to keep everyone from questioning you. I wouldn't say you and Callie were dating, more that you used her because you could."

Casey's mother gasped sharply and her eyes went wide. Casey didn't even look her way. She just pushed ahead. "Obviously, Callie is responsible for her own actions and she paid the ultimate price. She died of an overdose. I understand how she ended up going down that path. That she got injured in college and that's how she originally got prescribed pain medication. Like so many other people, she got addicted. When they told her she couldn't have it anymore, she looked for it elsewhere. In the end, the system failed her, like it failed so many other people and keeps failing them. But *you*," Her eyes darkened as she stared hard at Nathaniel. "You sold her drugs. You are the one who decided to play games with it, and make it as strong as you could. The more addicted people are, the more guaranteed customers you have. Right?"

Each word was sharp, like a barb. Casey's eyes were glittering with tears. She was fierce, so fierce. She looked away from Nathaniel. I squeezed her hand again, trying to impart what strength I could.

Casey's father had fallen quiet. His eyes kept circling the table and lingering on Nathaniel and Nathaniel's father. Casey's mother looked stricken.

Casey turned toward her, her eyes softening. "I know it hurts to hear this. I know that you want it to be something else. But this is what happened. Nathaniel knows this is what happened. I've talked to the police and I'll keep talking to the police. The part they don't know is that he threatened me." She turned to face her father. "He said he'll find a way to pin this on you. There were three people who saw Callie the night she died, Nathaniel and you and me. Because you stopped by to check on her. Nathaniel knows that I'd rather take the fall than you and that's how he's been trying to keep me quiet. I'm not sure what he thought he would get out of pretending he wanted to be involved with me." She rolled her eyes, her lips twisting in disgust.

Her focus turned back to Nathaniel. "I never really liked you. You were a jerk when we were kids, but our parents are best friends, so I had to put up with you. So did Callie. But you're gross. Callie didn't even like you, but she needed what you sold her." She finally brought her attention to Nathaniel's parents who had gotten mighty quiet. She looked between them.

"I don't know how much you know. David, I suspect you actually do know what happened. Even though I've always thought your son was a jerk, I didn't think you were. But I'm not going to stand back and let you take advantage of my parents. Dad, don't pay for Nathaniel's fucking attorney. He'll get a court appointed one and it will be fine. You're not in a position to do this. Is this why you're selling your house?" Her voice notched up with that question.

Casey's mother was crying. It appeared something finally got through to her because she stared at Nathaniel. "I can't believe you did this." At that, she stood and hurried away from the table.

Nathaniel was blustering about something. I sensed Casey wanted to leave, but I also realized we were in a bind here. Nathaniel was now ballpark five thousand miles from where he'd been charged. He could easily decide not to return.

As luck would have it, or something like that, Rex Masters, Willow Brook's police chief happened to be walking through the restaurant. I caught his eye and waved him over. I'd known Rex since I was a little kid with me and his son Cade being friends. My parents were also friends with him and his wife.

"What can I do for you, Leo?" Rex clapped his hand on my shoulder.

I didn't know how to explain why I wanted him to come over, but I sensed Rex quickly read the table, so to speak. Maybe he didn't know the details, but he knew he needed to hang close by. He began to ramble on about one thing after another, questioning Nathaniel's parents and Casey's dad about the Outer Banks in North Carolina, telling them about the best hiking trails here, and so on.

Within a few minutes, Susie returned to the table. When I introduced her to Rex, she perked up a little bit. Completely ignoring everyone else at the table, she asked, "You're the police chief here?"

"Yes, ma'am," Rex said with a nod.

"Well, this man lied to us." She gestured to Nathaniel. "As a result, we've accidentally lied to the court back in North Carolina. I definitely don't want to get in trouble for that. We would very much appreciate your assistance in this matter."

"Now, wait just a minute, Susie," David interjected. "We haven't done anything wrong."

"Yes, you have." Her southern twang carried a strong whiff of don't-fuck-with-me.

"John and I assured the court that we would be responsible for Nathaniel while he was out of state. We *never* would've agreed to this if we knew he had threatened Casey."

Nathaniel, being more of an idiot than I thought up to this fucked up point, stood from the table and ran out of the restaurant.

Chapter Thirty-Nine

CASEY

"Mom!" I jumped up, racing behind her when she leapt up from the table and began following Nathaniel.

I felt Leo right behind me. "Casey!" He caught me by the hand. "Hold up. Let me get your mom."

Fortunately, the restaurant was crowded. That slowed Nathaniel down, along with my mom, who seemed downright determined to catch up to him. As I looked ahead, I saw a group of firefighters clustered beside the bar, including Parker, Cade, Graham, and Hudson. There was also another police officer, Tanner McAdams, who I knew from the café.

I heard Rex call out to Tanner. He moved quickly and cut in front of Nathaniel's path, stopping him. My mom caught up to the group just as Leo and I reached her. "Mom, let the police handle this," I said quickly.

She ignored me and promptly kicked Nathaniel in the balls. He cried out in pain and bent over with a groan.

Everyone nearby glanced at her in shock.

"Well, it's effective." My mother's tone was pointed as she rested her hands on her hips.

"You're not wrong," Leo offered dryly while Nathaniel continued groaning.

When Nathaniel straightened up, his eyes were watering from the pain. He glanced around, his gaze landing on my mom. "I want to press assault charges," he choked out.

Calm as you please, Rex glanced from my mom to me and Leo, his brows arching up in question. "How about you fill me in on why you bolted from the table?"

Nathaniel's gaze went flat and he pressed his lips in a line. "I'm not talking to anybody, not until I have a lawyer."

"You're not under arrest at the moment," Rex said, his tone dry as burnt toast.

"He's under indictment for felony charges related to dealing drugs in North Carolina," I said quickly. "I can get the officer handling the case on the phone if you'd like. What my mom said at the table is true. He had to get permission to travel and my parents had to agree to supervise him."

Rex dipped his chin in acknowledgment. "Okay, then. Let's go back to the station." He turned toward Nathaniel, his gaze measuring. "You are currently being detained until we sort this out. Do I need to put you in handcuffs?"

Nathaniel's parents had reached us, along with my dad, in the circle around Nathaniel and my mom. For a moment, it looked like Nathaniel wanted to argue the point, but he finally let out a heavy sigh. "Let's go. I'll ride with my parents."

Rex shook his head sharply. "Oh no, you won't. You're riding with me."

"Oh, for fuck's sake," Nathaniel muttered.

We followed Rex and Tanner out in a slow-moving group. My mother wouldn't even make eye contact with David. As I studied Nathaniel's mother, I realized that she might be the only one among the three of them who had no idea what had really happened. She looked horrified. Meanwhile, David appeared resigned and guarded.

With Leo driving and my parents riding with us, we went to the police station. By the time we arrived, Rex and Tanner had taken Nathaniel in the back with Nathaniel's parents. After a few minutes, Maisie Steele came out from the back. "I'm gonna put you in the conference room while we wait."

After she escorted us into the back and offered us coffee, she pulled Leo and me aside. "I heard the update. They're going to hold him until they confer with law enforcement in North Carolina. Based on the charges, I don't think he's going to be released."

She gave me a quick hug. "It's going to be okay. I'd sit with you, but," she tapped her headset, "I've gotta stay on duty up front."

After she left, Leo sat beside me and reached for my hand under the table, giving me a reassuring squeeze.

My mother looked at me. "I'm sorry, honey." She burst into tears.

I stood up and rounded the table to give her a hug. Straightening, I handed her a tissue from the box in the center of the table. "Mom, none of this is your fault. The only part I knew for sure was that Callie was getting her drugs from Nathaniel and that they were kind of dating. He suspected I knew the rest. I think he tried to pressure me into getting involved with him because he hoped that would keep me in line. When Officer Blankenship reached out to me, everything I suspected turned out to be true."

"I'm so sorry. I miss Callie. I wish we could bring her back somehow." My mother took a shaky breath and blew her nose, while my dad stood up to give me a long hug.

After that, I sat back down and explained how I'd gotten suspicious about Nathaniel. "I knew Callie was having trouble. She told me she had it under control. I didn't know Nathaniel was purposefully giving her stronger drugs." I swiped at my tears with my fingertips. Leo circled his palm between my shoulder blades, his touch comforting me.

My dad looked at Leo. "Are you really her fiancé?"

Leo waited just long enough that I cut in. "I'd like him to be. He's really my boyfriend, and—" I looked over at my mom.

"Since you were trying so hard to sell me on Nathaniel, I needed a way to get you to back off. Honestly, I know that's stupid now. I should've just told you the whole story, but I didn't know if I could ever convince anyone of my suspicions. His mom has been your best friend since before I was born." I let out a heavy sigh as the enormity of what Nathaniel had done struck me anew.

My dad reached for my mom's hand. "I don't think his mom knew."

"You don't?"

Leo chimed in, "That's not what I'm reading from her either. His dad knew something. Maybe he didn't know the whole story, but I think he knew enough of it. They've been banking on you, literally, to pay his attorney bills."

My dad narrowed his eyes. "I already texted the attorney that we are no longer covering any bills. They can pay for it themselves." He shook his head before leveling his gaze with mine. "I'm sorry for this whole mess too. Your mom always thought it would be so perfect if Nathaniel married one of our kids. We should've trusted you and let it be. We got swept up in grief."

The relief I felt at the whole truth being out there lifted an immense weight off my shoulders. We didn't have to wait much longer before Rex came in and updated us that they were holding Nathaniel until they made arrangements to transport him back to North Carolina.

He shifted his focus to my mom. "I'm not gonna charge you, but..." Rex shook his head. "Next time, try to refrain from kicking him in the balls."

My mom was unabashed. "He was trying to run away and that was an effective way to stop him," she said tartly.

A month or so later

"Okay, now, we need to adjust that." I pointed to the speed setting on the kitchen stand mixer.

Dora was standing beside me on a stool while we were in the kitchen making cookies.

It was Thursday night, my first night here when Dora was here. Leo had gone into town to pick up pizza at Dora's request.

"What's the setting?" she asked.

"About there." I pointed to the center.

She carefully adjusted it, and we watched as the cookie dough hook spun slowly.

A few minutes later, Dora was carefully shaping the dough into balls and placing them on a baking tray when Leo came walking into the kitchen. Dora was so focused on what she was doing, she didn't initially notice him. He caught my eyes and waggled his brows as a slow grin stretched across his face.

My belly did a little flip and heat spun through me like little sparklers. *Mmmmm.* I kept wondering if my hormones would ever chill out around him. All evidence thus far didn't indicate they would. It only seemed to get worse.

You'll get over it. You can't think he's this hot forever, my cynical mind chimed in.

My hormones shouted that train of thought down.

Leo held up a grocery bag. "I got the powdered sugar, as requested."

Dora beamed. "Do we roll them in the powdered sugar now?"

I shook my head as I took the bag from Leo. "We do that after they've baked."

"Since we're making wedding cookies, does that mean you're getting married soon?" Dora asked, her eyes bouncing from me to Leo with a sly smile. Dora might be only six, but she had opinions.

Flustered, I laughed a little. "Um, you picked out the kind of cookies we're making," I pointed out.

Leo slid his arm around my waist and gave me a subtle squeeze.

Dora shrugged. "I was just asking."

Leo stopped beside her to inspect the tray of cookies. She shooed him away when he offered to help. He grinned, tugging lightly on her ponytail as he stepped back and rested his hips against the counter.

"Where's the pizza?" Dora asked.

"Oh crap! It's in the backseat. Be right back."

A short while later, we were enjoying pizza while the cookies baked. I was a little nervous because this was my first official "slumber party" as Dora insisted on calling it. We'd had a careful conversation with her about it. Leo had explained to her that he cared about me and wanted me to be part of his life. Every so often, I wondered about the boundaries her mother had set around these things because Dora straight up asked us if we were going to have a "birds and bees" night.

While I thought my face might melt off, Leo had nearly choked with that question, but he'd kept it together and asked her what she meant. She'd said her mom told her that's how babies were made. She proceeded to request that we make a little brother.

When the cookies were ready, Leo took on the assignment of helping her learn how to roll the baked cookies in the powdered sugar. Dora ate the first one and let out a little happy sigh with Leo enthusing, "These are the best cookies I ever had."

After she went to bed, Leo came out to the living room, walking so quietly I didn't even hear him until he whispered, "Casey."

I glanced over to see him holding a finger to his lips. He sat down beside me and let out a heartfelt sigh. "Bedtime can be tough. I figured tonight might be a challenge since you're here, but she fell asleep. How you doing?" He scooted closer and curled his arm around my shoulders.

I smiled up at him. "Good. I've been nervous all night, honestly."

He angled to face me. "What are you nervous about?"

My heart started to kick a little faster and my belly felt all ticklish. When I felt his thumb sliding back and forth in a slow caress along the edge of my collarbone, my skin got hot and tingles radiated from that strip of skin. He wasn't even trying to turn me on, but my body felt like an antenna, tuned solely to the frequency of Leo.

I forced myself to focus and took a quick breath. "I know we've talked about things, but this is a big night. Staying here when Dora is here feels like a big deal."

His gaze sobered. "There's been a lot going on."

I snorted. "Seriously. I'm relieved the truth came out with my parents, and I'm sorry it got so crazy."

"You don't have anything to apologize for. I wanted to be there for you through all of it. I'm just really grateful it's okay. You don't have to carry this alone anymore and your parents believe you about what happened with Callie."

Nathaniel had been flown back to North Carolina, this time

under arrest because of the threats he'd made to me. My father was no longer helping pay for his attorney. Whether or not Nathaniel's father knew exactly what happened with Callie, it was clear he had known more than Nathaniel's mother did. She was furious with both of them and had moved out. My parents' house had sold, and they'd moved into a retirement community.

I could never fix everything that happened, but at least the people who mattered the most were okay and Callie would get justice.

Leo tipped his head to the side as he studied me, his thumb driving me wild with subtle strokes over my collarbone. I finally reached up and put my hand over his. "You're distracting me."

His lips curled in a slow smile that sent my belly into a spin. "I haven't had a chance to say something important."

"What's that?"

He suddenly looked a little nervous and his shoulders rose with a deep breath. "I already told you this, but it was a hectic moment, so I want to say it again. I love you. I'd love to make our fake engagement real."

My heart felt like it might burst out of my chest as joy rose in a crashing cacophony through me. "I love you." I leaned up to pepper his face with kisses.

"I love you too," he murmured against my cheek. "What do you think? Will you marry me?"

I blinked before I burst into tears.

"Hey, hey, that wasn't supposed to make you cry." Leo reached for a napkin from the stack on the coffee table.

"They're not sad tears. It's just a lot of emotion. Of course I'll marry you. Yes, yes, yes!"

Leo's smile was slow, while my heart kept on beating hard and fast and true. "I planned to ask you to marry me, I just didn't know when. I don't have a ring yet."

I giggled. "We haven't done anything in the right order, so it makes sense you don't have a ring yet."

"We're gonna fake it true," he teased and I giggled again.

He tugged me into his lap. We tumbled into kisses that were slow and teasing. Leo kindled the fire burning inside with every stroke of his tongue and brush of his lips.

I felt as if I were falling. We stumbled into the bedroom. By the time we were close to naked, and I was straddling him, it felt as if a storm were rushing through me—that familiar sense of need and want tangling within the intimacy I experienced with him.

"Casey, look at me, sweetheart," he rasped.

I lifted my eyes to meet his, my heart pounding fast and true. He palmed my cheek. I felt his crown at my entrance just before he said, "I love you."

He filled me in a slow thrust upward as I sank down over him, sheathing him in the very core of me. I could barely speak as I whispered, "I love you too."

I was spun with him into the center of the fire that burned hot and fast and always overtook me. When I came through in the aftermath of a body-shaking climax, I felt washed clean. The way the air felt after a storm—a startling contrast of crisp freshness, as if everything was starting anew.

I breathed in his scent, musky with a hint of woodsy, and felt my lips curling into a smile. Simply being with him like this made my body, heart, and soul smile.

Leo sifted his fingers through my hair and I felt the rumble of his voice when he rasped my name. "Casey?"

"Yeah?"

Chapter Forty-One

LEO

Casey was soft and warm where she rested against me. I could feel her heartbeat pounding along with mine. I felt one last gust of her breath across my collarbone before she lifted her head from where it was tucked against my shoulder.

"Yeah?" she repeated.

My lips tugged into a smile. "I don't remember what I was gonna say," I said honestly.

She giggled and the sound curled around my heart. Her gaze sobered and she bit her lip. "Was I loud? I hope I didn't wake Dora up."

I bit back another laugh. "I doubt it. It's usually only the first few minutes after she falls asleep that I have to worry about her waking up."

The reality of being a father slammed into my chest, as it was wont to do every so often.

"What is it?" Casey pressed.

"Every so often, I realize I'm a dad and that I know Dora well enough now to know something like that." I shook my head in wonder. "It's a little crazy."

Casey's smile was slow and warm. She lifted her hand, trailing her thumb along the stubbled edge of my jaw. "You're a really good dad and I'm glad Dora is with you."

———

The following morning when I woke up with Casey curled up beside me, my heart felt full. I wanted to linger in bed with her. I wanted to tug her into the shower with me and tease her to another climax.

Alas, that wasn't to be and I knew it. Dora was an early riser and more energetic than the average adult, and specifically me. I gave myself a few minutes of bliss to rest with Casey and pressed a lingering kiss on the side of her neck before I forced myself out of bed. Casey was already awake as well and got up with me.

When she stood there with one of my T-shirts hanging down around her thighs and her hair tousled around her shoulders, it was all I could do not to drag her back into bed. "Do I have time for a quick shower?" she asked.

I whisked my gaze toward the clock beside the bed. "We've got a few minutes."

Casey's eyes widened. "Let's go for it!" She dashed into the bathroom.

Roughly ten minutes later, we were toweling off, and I grinned over at her. "If Dora's awake, I'm blaming that on you," I teased her.

We could've showered in five minutes, except when I couldn't will my arousal away, Casey curled her palm around my length.

She giggled and yanked on her clothes. "I'll start coffee."

After she hurried out, I chuckled at my reflection in the mirror. I looked downright giddy.

When I walked out to the kitchen a few minutes later, Dora was talking at full-speed to Casey about otters. She grabbed Casey by the hand to pull her over to the windows to show her a moose and two calves standing in the field outside. Casey was more alert than me at this hour, but seeing as she often went into work at the coffee shop over an hour earlier, that made sense. As I watched them, my heart felt so full it ached.

Dora turned toward me and beamed. "Daddy!" That tightness in my chest eased, my heart feeling cracked wide-open as if sunlight were pouring directly into it.

Dora ran across the room. She hugged me briefly, but she didn't linger. She caught my hand. "We're making scrambled eggs."

My gaze arced over to Casey who was following us. This was one night, and I knew I couldn't start playing house with Casey. And yet, it was the first step in the direction I knew I wanted to go.

Dora let go of my hand to open the door to the refrigerator, calling out, "How many eggs should I get out?"

Casey stopped beside me, her eyes crinkling at the corners with her smile. "What do you think? Eight?"

"Yeah. Trust me, we'll finish them."

Casey giggled and started to move away. I curled my arm around her waist. Dora was preoccupied with counting out the eggs. "Can we really do this?" I asked.

Casey smiled at me. "We already are."

EPILOGUE

Luna Talton

A gust of salty air blew my hair wild. I lifted a hand to catch it and smooth it back. I looked out over the water, marveling at the view. The mountains towered in the distance and the sun struck sparks off the ocean's surface. Even though I'd grown up in Alaska, it never failed to wow me. Whenever people told me they didn't believe in any kind of spirituality, I would tell them they just needed to go to Alaska. Because it was truly a spiritual experience. Nature here snatched your breath right out of your lungs and reminded you that the whole world was a cathedral.

"Luna!" My friend Casey's voice reached me and I spun around.

She was lugging a cooler all by herself and stumbled a little on the rock-strewn shoreline. I hurried over and reached for the other handle. "What's in here?" I asked.

"Food," she teased. "We have empty coolers too. Everyone tells me we have fish to catch. Have you ever done this?" she asked me as her gaze whisked over to several fishing nets propped up against another cooler nearby on the beach.

"Of course! Dipnetting is an Alaskan tradition. If you grow up here, you have to do it. I can't even imagine not doing it."

After we set the cooler down, I opened it to peer inside. "Oh wow, you didn't mess around." When I glanced up at Casey, she grinned. "Well, you said we might be here all day."

Someone called her name. She looked over her shoulder, a smile stretching across her face. Her cheeks went pink when I chimed in, "You are so in love."

She shrugged. "I am. And, it's really the best thing ever."

I impulsively hugged her. "Everyone deserves love like what you and Leo have," I said just before her boyfriend reached us.

"Hey, Luna," Leo said, stopping beside us. "Ready to net some salmon?"

"Absolutely!"

Leo chuckled, holding two fishing nets aloft. "I have two options for nets. There's my favorite, which is the cedar handle. I also brought a stainless steel one."

Casey studied the nets before her gaze bounced to me. "People are *really* into the nets for this. I can't dipnet yet. I haven't been here a full year yet."

"You can watch. It's fun," I replied.

I glanced around the area. Seagulls were calling raucously in the air, and I could hear the distant screech of an eagle. We were at the Kenai River in Alaska, a favorite destination for dipnetting. The activity was aptly named. You gathered on the shoreline at the edge of the water with handheld fishing nets to catch the salmon swimming upriver. Some people chose to dipnet with nets dangling over the edge of boats, but I'd always preferred to be on the shoreline. We were near the mouth of the river, where the fish came rushing in from the ocean in a race to spawn before they died. If they didn't get scooped up in a net, they would spawn and die.

The beach was getting crowded. There were regulations for the size of the nets and just about everyone had an opinion on the best nets.

I started to suit up in my neoprene fishing waders. Casey looked around, commenting, "This is crazy!"

"What do you mean?" I asked as I stepped into my wading boots.

"You and Leo told me about it, and Maisie was telling me—" Casey turned away as Maisie called out a greeting. We waved back and Casey continued, "I guess I didn't realize there would be this many people. Parking is practically a competitive sport."

I grinned. "It's awesome. Fun though it is, it's serious. People rely on the salmon they catch here to feed their families. One person can get up to twenty-five salmon with an additional ten salmon for each family member. That's a lot of food. Not to mention how fresh Alaskan silver salmon is." I tapped my fingers together in the motion for a chef's kiss.

Maisie reached us with Amelia, Lucy, Tish, Griffin, and more trailing behind her. Recently, I'd started to feel like the odd one out. Many of my friends were happily married or coupled up, and I was still very single. I couldn't even imagine being anything but single.

"Hey, Parker," Griffin called.

My eyes instantly swung in his direction, while I ordered my hormones to ignore Parker Reeves. I also studiously ignored the inconvenient embarrassment that he didn't recognize me. *It was ten years ago. Forget about it.*

"Hey, hey," Parker said with a lopsided grin when he stopped by our group.

"Is this your first year dipnetting?" Casey asked him.

Parker shook his head. "No, ma'am," he teased. "I might have only moved to Willow Brook in the last year, but I am a born and bred Alaskan."

"Well, I'm gonna watch and learn. Show me your net," Casey said.

Beck stopped beside Maisie. "That sounds a little inappropriate, Casey," he teased with an exaggerated brow waggle.

Casey rolled her eyes. "Look, this is my first time watching this. Everybody keeps talking about their nets, so I'm trying to understand why they're so important."

Parker's grin sent sparks pinwheeling inside of me. "A lot of people build their own nets." He gestured to the net I was holding. "I'm on team-Luna. I like them with a cedar handle and a rectangular net. The cedar floats in the water, so it makes those easy to hold."

Casey nodded along. "Hmm. I guess I have until next year to figure out what kind of net I want."

The beach was getting more and more crowded. Amelia caught my eye. "I like the cedar handle too because it floats."

Beck chimed in, "Well, now there are advantages to the stainless-steel ones because your grip slides more easily if you need to adjust it."

"You undercut your own point. If your hands can slide easier, you can lose your grip," Maisie pointed out. Maisie stopped beside Casey, pulling her into a side hug. "I was new at this too, but I've done it for a few years now and it's really fun. You're gonna love it when you get to go next year."

"I sure love salmon, so I'm looking forward to it." She glanced toward me, worry creasing her brow. "I can eat the salmon Leo catches, right?"

I burst out laughing. "Of course, you just have to officially be a resident before you can get a dipnetting permit."

"Did you get a king salmon tag?" Amelia asked me.

I gave her a thumbs-up. "Sure did!"

It wasn't long before we were all wading into the ocean. I tended to push the envelope on this and go as far out as I could. I loved the feeling of the water rushing against me. Today, the fish were coming in fast and I could feel them bouncing against my legs. I had almost caught my limit when I waded back into the water to try to catch one more salmon.

The sun was high in the sky, and the wind was starting to pick up so the water was getting choppy. I didn't think much of it when a boat came rolling down the river. The boat's wake was high enough that my feet lifted off the sandy bottom. I still didn't worry until several minutes ticked by and I realized I was drifting further away from the shoreline.

"Luna!"

I recognized Beck's voice and glanced back. "Yeah?"

"You okay?"

I wanted to tell him I was completely fine. I was independent, some people would probably think I was stubbornly so. I hated asking for help. Ever. But I didn't want to be stupid and I was deeply practical. I knew that if I didn't somehow change course, I might start drifting too far out into the current where the water could carry me out to sea. Literally.

The water was also cold. Alaska wasn't a place where people swam without a wetsuit, even on the hottest days of summer. That cold water was beginning to seep over the tops of my waders. I was smart though, and I was wearing a life jacket.

I glanced back at Beck and called out, "I'm not sure!"

I turned to face the shore so I could keep an eye on how fast I might be drifting away. I wasn't alone in this predicament. I could see another person, maybe fifty feet away, who was trying to swim directly back to shore. I knew that wasn't the best move. It was safer to swim at an angle across the current.

I was a strong swimmer, but I had a fishing net in hand and was wearing waders that were starting to fill with water. I did the only practical thing I could do. I kept a hold of the net because it was floating, but I began to kick with my feet and unbuckle the tops of my wader straps. After I got them off, I turned them upside down so the water drained out and hooked the boots under my armpits. When I glanced toward the shoreline again, I noticed it was further away.

There were voices calling to those of us who had gotten swept away due to the boat's wake.

"Don't panic, Luna," I said to myself. "You're going to be fine."

I was starting to shiver. I kept my eyes on the shore and began to swim, letting go of my net finally. Only a moment later as I was starting to despair, a small boat approached and someone called my name.

When I looked over, I saw Parker and Griffin in the boat. Parker caught my eye. "We're cutting the engine and I'm going to get you out of there."

Parker slowly reached a hand out, saying, "Just grab my hand, Luna. I've got you."

Cold as I was, my hands felt numb so it was difficult to hold on. Parker's grip was strong and he kept a firm hold on me as he reached for my other arm. He lifted me into the boat, scooping me in his strong arms. I didn't realize my teeth were chattering until I tried to talk.

"I didn't kn-kn-kn-know..."

"Wait to talk," Parker said. He held me in his protective embrace.

With it being so crowded and busy, I couldn't even remember when I'd last seen him on the beach. He was in jeans and a T-shirt. I savored the feel of his warmth. Griffin leaned into the water to get my net and tossed it over the side of the boat. I glanced over to see another boat had gone to rescue the two other people who had drifted out.

"All right, I'm headed to shore," Griffin said.

"You have any blankets on board?" Parker asked.

Griffin pointed to a seat. Parker kept an arm around me as he leaned over and opened it to pull out a big blanket. A moment later, he wrapped it around me.

"You don't have to keep holding me," I finally managed when I could catch my breath.

When he glanced down and my eyes locked with his, every-thing felt suspended. My heart thumped hard against my ribs, the beat of it echoing. It was as if a pebble of fire dropped into a pond and rippled through me. I became acutely aware of the feeling of his palm curled on the edge of my hip.

"We need to get you warm," he said.

PARKER

Luna blinked up at me. Her big blue eyes were wide and her dark curls were pulled up in a ponytail. Her teeth were still chattering when she replied, "I-I-I…"

She clenched her jaw, shaking her head as if in annoyance with herself for being cold. "I'm fine," she ground out through clenched teeth.

"Luna, that water isn't much above fifty degrees. A quick way to get hypothermia is to swim in the ocean in Alaska in the summer. It's pretty efficient," I said dryly.

I reached for the towel I'd gotten with the blanket and handed it to her. She dabbed at her face with it before almost burrowing into herself. "You might have a point," she said a moment later.

Her teeth had stopped chattering, but she was still shivering. "It was that boat wake," she said.

"Yeah, three people got carried out. How many fish did you get so far?"

"Twenty-four. I should've stopped."

I chuckled when I looked down at her again. Her shivering was slowing. At that moment, my heart gave a resounding kick and awareness struck me like a fiery bolt.

Luna was curled against me in a soft bundle. I wanted to hold her close, to protect her.

You want to do a lot more than protect her, my cynical mind chimed in.

Luna was cute, sexy, and downright delectable. I saw her just frequently enough that I had to make an effort not to notice her. She baked donuts for the local coffee shop, and she was friends with almost everybody I worked with. There was also something familiar about her. She reminded me of someone I'd met once. Just once, but the memory shined bright. Yet, Luna had crazy wild curls, while that someone had stick straight hair and a different name. I told myself again that it was just a fluke.

"Do you want to drop your net in now and catch one more?" I managed to ask.

She glanced around. "How far until we get to the boat ramp?"

Griffin glanced over. "A few minutes. How are you doing?" he called over the sound of the motor.

"Getting warmer."

"We need to get you some dry clothes," I commented.

Luna let out a little sigh. "When I was little, my mom always used to tell me that I shouldn't go too far out. Lesson learned." She rolled her eyes.

I chuckled. "Nobody was gonna let you drift out to sea."

"Thank you very much for stopping. You were on the beach earlier. When did you decide to go out in a boat?"

"Well, it was pretty crowded and Griffin texted me that he had his boat, so I went over to meet him."

After a beat, she nodded. "You can't get swept away if you're in the boat."

"True," I agreed.

"I'm think I'm warm," she said.

"Would you like to keep the blanket?" I asked as I reluctantly eased my hold on her.

"Please. I'm still wet, so without it, I'll get cold fast."

"You didn't lose a thing," I pointed out, gesturing to the net and her waders. "Smart move to take those off."

She shrugged. "They were filling with water. I'm glad you all caught my net for me."

She let the blanket fall down around her waist before tucking the ends of it to hold it in place. My eyes dipped down to notice her T-shirt was damp. I forced my eyes back up before they lingered too long.

I cleared my throat before standing up and handing her the handle to her net. "Drop that in the water. You can get that last fish."

She tucked the handle to the net in a holder and let the net drag through the water by the boat. Minutes later, she let out a happy squeal when a fish swam into her net. She dragged it into the boat and started jumping up and down. "It's a king!

She quickly freed it from the net and held it up to show it off. Griffin threw a grin over his shoulder as he steered the boat toward the ramp.

When I looked over at Luna again, she was covered in sand with a few streaks of fish blood on her arms from a busy day of catching, gutting, and cleaning fish. Her curls blew in a wild riot around her shoulders, and all I could think was that I wanted her.

Thank you for reading Casey & Leo's story! Want a glimpse of the future for them? Join my newsletter to receive an exclusive scene.

Sign up here: https://BookHip.com/TPPTARR

p.s. If you are already subscribed, you'll still be able to access the scene.

Up next is in the Wild Fire Series is Only Ever You.

I never thought I'd see Parker again.

It probably doesn't make sense to say I lied for a good reason, but I swear I did. I never thought I'd see Parker again.

Until he rescues me from almost getting swept out to sea, quite literally. He's growly, grumpy and sexy. He also doesn't recognize me.

Don't miss Luna & Parker's swoony, emotional and protective second chance romance!

One-click: Only Ever You- due out November 2025!

For more swoon & sass...

This Crazy Love kicks off the Swoon Series - small town southern romance with enough heat to melt you! Jackson & Shay's story is epic - swoon-worthy & intensely emotional. Jackson just happens to be Shay's brother's best friend. He's also *seriously* easy on the eyes. Shay has a past, the kind of past she would most definitely like to forget. Past or not, Jackson is about to rock her world. Don't miss their story!

Burn For Me is a second chance romance for the ages. Sexy firefighters? Check. Rugged men? Check. Wrapped up together? Check. Brave the fire in this hot, small-town romance. Amelia & Cade were high school sweethearts & then it all fell apart. When they cross paths again, it's epic - don't miss Cade's story!

For more small town romance, take a visit to Last Frontier Lodge in Diamond Creek. A sexy, alpha SEAL meets his match with a brainy heroine in Take Me Home. Marley is all brains & Gage is all brawn. Sparks fly when their worlds collide. Don't miss Gage & Marley's story!

If sports romance lights your spark, check out The Play. Liam is a British footballer who falls for Olivia, his doctor. A twist of forbidden heats up this swoon-worthy & laugh-out-loud romance. Don't miss Liam & Olivia's story.

Be sure to sign up for my newsletter for the latest news, teasers & more! Click here to sign up: http://jhcroixauthor.com/subscribe/

Wild Fire Series
All The Afters

When We Dare
Fake It True
Only Ever You - coming soon!
Fireweed Harbor Series
Make You Mine
Dare To Fall
Be The One
One More Time
Wait For You
Ever After All
Light My Fire Series
Wild With You
Hold Me Now
Only Ever Us
Fall For Me
Keep Me Close
With Every Breath
All It Takes
Take Me Now
Meant To Be
Dare With Me Series
Crash Into You
Evers & Afters
Come To Me
Back To Us
Take Me There
After We Fall
Swoon Series
This Crazy Love
Wait For Me
Break My Fall
Truly Madly Mine
Still Go Crazy
If We Dare
Steal My Heart

Into The Fire Series
Burn For Me
Slow Burn
Burn So Bad
Hot Mess
Burn So Good
Sweet Fire
Play With Fire
Melt With You
Burn For You
Crash & Burn
That Snowy Night
Haven's Bay Holiday Series
All I Want
All I Need
All We Have
All We Are
Brit Boys Sports Romance
The Play
Big Win
Out Of Bounds
Play Me
Naughty Wish
Diamond Creek Alaska Novels
When Love Comes
Follow Love
Love Unbroken
Love Untamed
Tumble Into Love
Christmas Nights
Lodge Series
Take Me Home
Love at Last
Just This Once
Falling Fast

<u>Stay With Me</u>
<u>When We Fall</u>
<u>Hold Me Close</u>
<u>Crazy For You</u>
<u>Just Us</u>

ACKNOWLEDGMENTS

My gratitude for my readers grows with every book. Whether you are a brand-new-to-my-books reader or whether you've read every story, please know words aren't enough to capture how much it means to have a reader take a chance on my stories. Thank you for the journey.

Virginia Tesi Carey edited Leo & Casey's story graciously and kept me on track with it. My proofreader, Terri D., should probably just remind me time isn't as flexible as my stories might show. She is patient and kind about catching my mistakes. My early readers sweep up any lingering mistakes, and I'm so thankful.

Najla Qamber keeps making magic with these covers, and I love them so. So many thanks to my assistant, Erin. Seriously. Much gratitude to my publicist, Danielle Sanchez, for so much feedback behind the scenes.

To one sweet dog who reminds me every day what unconditional love is and that our morning runs are required. To DBC for giving me the time and space to write.

xoxo

J.H. Croix

ABOUT THE AUTHOR

USA Today Bestselling Author J. H. Croix lives in a small town with her husband and just one spoiled dog. Croix writes contemporary romance with sassy women and alpha men who aren't afraid to show some emotion. Her love for quirky small-towns and the characters that inhabit them shines through in her writing. When she's not writing, you can find her cooking, counting the birds in her backyard, and running with her dog, which is when her best plotting happens.

Places you can find me:
jhcroixauthor.com
jhcroix@jhcroix.com

facebook.com/jhcroix
instagram.com/jhcroix
bookbub.com/authors/j-h-croix

www.ingramcontent.com/pod-product-compliance
Lightning Source LLC
Chambersburg PA
CBHW020802310726
48969CB00002B/661